EAT, PREY, LOVE

AN ANNABELLE ARCHER WEDDING PLANNER MYSTERY

LAURA DURHAM

BROADMOOR BOOKS

FREE DOWNLOAD!

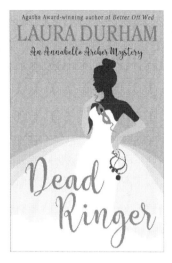

This book is dedicated to the lovely friends I made in Bali who inspired me to write this book, the beautiful island of Bali, and the Balinese people. Special thanks to Walt, Art, Mary Frances, Brian, Kristen, Albert, Phillip, Amanda, Ilana, Joe, Christian, Sam, Katie, Hope, Ivy, and many more for letting me borrow tidbits of you to fictionalize. All the bad guys and victims are completely fabricated because I couldn't bear to kill off any of you!

EAT, PREY, LOVE

An Annabelle Archer Wedding Planner Mystery

By Laura Durham

CHAPTER 1

I dropped my black carry-on bag in the foyer of the hotel suite and rubbed the deep groove it had left in my shoulder. Next time I wouldn't pack so much for the plane, I told myself. Not that I'd be getting on another thirty-plus hour flight anytime soon.

The trip from Washington, DC, to Bali, Indonesia, had gone through New York and Taiwan before reaching the exotic island that would be home for the next week. It had taken over a day of travel to arrive, and I could feel the exhaustion begin to overtake me as I followed my Balinese room butler while he gave me a tour of the spacious suite.

"Your living and dining room, Ms. Archer," the man said, sweeping an arm to encompass the beige-and-teakwood furniture that decorated the room. A large round mirror hung over a table that held an arrangement of white orchids and a russet-colored urn with a lid.

I took a quick peek at myself in the mirror. Aside from the fact that my long auburn hair hadn't been washed in almost two days, and most of my makeup had worn off, I didn't look as tired as I felt. "Call me Annabelle."

"Okay, Ms. Annabelle." The man grinned and swept an arm in the direction of the flat-screen TV on a polished-wood console. I lifted the fresh-flower garland from around my neck and placed it on the round dining table beside a glass bowl of tropical fruits, feeling my stomach growl at the sight of the food. When had I last eaten? At this point, the meals on the airplane were a blur of blandness. I ran my hand over the bumpy green skin of a small fruit I'd never seen before and wondered if it would be sweet or tart.

"Your bedroom and closet, Ms. Annabelle." The butler led me from the living room to the bedroom with a king-sized bed covered in white linens with huge wall mirrors to each side. This room, like the first one, had one entire wall of glass that looked out onto the balcony and was covered with beige linen drapes. He pulled open the drapes and light poured into the room.

I blinked at the brightness and made a mental note to close the curtains before I changed. I then poked my head into the walk-in closet with a series of blond wood drawers beneath the long hanging racks on two sides. "This is larger than some apartments in Georgetown."

The butler smiled again and nodded. I fell in step behind him as he showed me the final room—the marble and glass bathroom with a sleek freestanding tub at one end, broken up by a long stretch of countertop and double sinks before the glass-enclosed shower at the other. I opened a frosted-glass door next to the shower and the lid of a modern-looking toilet rose automatically.

"It's motion activated," the butler explained, waving his hand up and down to demonstrate how to raise and lower the lid. "And the seat is heated. You have a control panel to the side."

Wow, I mouthed.

The butler gestured to the glass wall at the far end of the bathroom. "The hot tub is outside on the balcony. You let me know when you want to use it, and I will remove the cover and turn it on for you."

I looked at him. "I have my own hot tub?"

The dark-haired man smiled and nodded. He seemed pleased by how impressed I was with the suite. "Would you like to use it now?"

I waved away the thought. "No, not now. I should unpack first."

He bobbed his head and smiled some more. "If you need anything at all, you call me."

I followed him back through the suite, tipping him with American dollars since I hadn't had the chance to change money yet. He seemed pleased as he closed the front door of the room behind him, although I suspected he would have smiled even if he'd been disappointed. So far the Balinese people had impressed me as the happiest people I'd ever met. Certainly they smiled the most.

I took a deep breath, enjoying being alone in my room after such a long time in a plane surrounded by people. I slid off my black cardigan and draped it over the back of a teak wood chair as I crossed the living room and pulled open the sliding glass door that led to the balcony. The long marble balcony stretched the entire length of my suite with a covered sunken hot tub at the far end and a collection of dark brown and cream lounge furniture topped with orange throw pillows that filled the remaining space. As tasteful as the furniture was, it was the view that had me catching my breath.

Standing at the glass balcony wall, I could see the blue of the Indian Ocean in front of me, blocked only by clusters of tall palm trees and one of the hotel pools dotted with lounge chairs at its edge as it ran the length of the resort. To my right, ivory curtain-draped cabanas sat along the side of the pool, and I could hear a few people splashing around in the clear water. I looked past the pool to the cliff that jutted out into the ocean and spotted a multi-tier Balinese temple perched on the edge. It reminded me of a wedding cake with its white layers getting progressively smaller until it reached a point at the top. As the owner of Wedding

Belles, one of Washington DC's top wedding planning companies, I had weddings on my mind more than most people.

I took a deep breath, smelling the faint scent of salt water and feeling my shoulders relax. I sat down on the nearest lounge chair and stretched my feet out in front of me, letting my head drop back against the cushion and closing my eyes. I breathed in slowly and tried to let the plane trip melt away.

"Can you believe this place?" Kate's voice jerked me out of my moment's peace. My assistant's head was leaning over the divide between my suite and hers, her blond bob moving in the breeze.

"It's pretty amazing," I said.

She took in my balcony and nodded in approval. "You have a hot tub, too. I'm going to come over and check out your place."

Her head disappeared before I could tell her that our rooms were probably identical, so I reluctantly rose from the lounge chair and walked to my front door as the doorbell chimed.

"Don't you love the fact that we have doorbells?" she asked when I'd opened the door. "It's probably because you wouldn't hear someone knocking if you were all the way in the bedroom or bathroom. Speaking of bathrooms, can you believe that shower? Our entire crew could fit inside." She lowered her voice as if an imaginary person might overhear us. "And the toilet seat is heated."

I was amazed that Kate had as much energy as she did after our long trip and lack of sleep. I was also surprised that she'd already changed out of her leggings and hoodie from the plane and was wearing a pink-and-white sundress that, per usual, showed plenty of leg. "The hotel is spoiling us; that's for sure."

Kate kicked off her pink kitten heels, leaving them behind in the foyer. "I mean, we've been on FAM trips before, but this is incredible."

I had to agree. As wedding planners, we'd been invited to stay overnight and familiarize ourselves with various hotels and resorts (the phrase "FAM trip" was short for "familiarization trip"), but never had we been invited to Bali and put up in suites in a luxury oceanfront resort that had been named one of the top in the world.

"When do you think we meet the other people on the trip?" Kate asked as she flopped down on my couch and tucked her bare feet under her.

I shrugged. "The official events don't begin until tonight's dinner."

"Did you see the attendee map they emailed us? There are planners here from Paris, Australia, and Japan. It's so cool that we're the only planners from DC."

I didn't want to tell Kate that I'd been a little intimidated when I'd seen the list of the forty other planners, florists, and caterers who would be joining us. One of the LA planners had even had his own reality show.

"Don't worry, Annabelle." Kate seemed to read my mind. "We're just as fabulous as the rest of the people here. Our Rose Garden wedding was featured in *Insider Weddings* magazine just last month."

"And I'm sure that's one of the reasons we're here," I said, joining her on the couch and lifting the glass dome off a plate of miniature sweets on the coffee table. "The owners of the magazine are co-sponsoring the trip."

"Booking that White House wedding definitely made up for some of our past disasters." Kate took a mini tart topped with tropical fruits when I held out the plate.

"I hope you don't go around telling people we have wedding disasters," I said, popping a tartlet in my mouth and sighing at the sweetness of the fruit and pastry cream.

Kate swallowed and dabbed at the edge of her mouth. "Well, what would you call the murders?"

I gave her my sternest look. "I would call them an off-limit topic of conversation on this trip."

She held up her hands. "Fine. You'll have to tell the rest of the gang, though. You know how Fern loves to gossip."

I thought this was rich coming from Kate since she was usually the person to whom our friend, and go-to wedding hairstylist, Fern loved gossiping.

Kate stood up and bounded out to the balcony. "Do you think we can see their rooms from ours?"

I followed her with a little less bounce in my step. "Maybe. They should all be on the same floor as us."

Kate craned herself over the glass barrier. "Fern, Richard, Buster, Mack!" She paused as she waited for a response, but no one answered.

"Maybe they don't have their balcony doors opened." I leaned my forearms against the glass and looked down on the pool area. "Richard looked pretty tired when we arrived. He might be taking a nap."

"And Buster and Mack said they needed to meet with the in-house floral department about tonight's design," Kate said. "How cool is it that they're going to be teaching the staff at the resort how to arrange flowers while we're here?"

"Apparently, the guys at *Insider Weddings* talked up their design for our Rose Garden wedding so much to the hotel manager that she insisted they come and teach her floral team," I said.

"They'll still be able to have fun with us, won't they?" Kate asked. "Although our schedule looks pretty packed, too."

"What schedule?" I asked.

Kate flung a hand in the direction of my bedroom. "There's an itinerary on the bed. Which reminds me, we're supposed to meet the group in the lobby for afternoon tea in about ten minutes."

I straightened up. "Ten minutes? Why didn't you tell me? No wonder you look so cute."

Kate winked at me. "Be honest, Annabelle. I always look cute."

Before I could respond, my eye caught a glimpse of a blond man in beige pants and a mango-colored shirt walking along the pool deck toward the hotel. Something about the way he walked made me pause, and I tried to get a better look as he vanished inside the building.

"Are you okay?" Kate asked. "You look like you've seen a ghost."

I shook my head, trying to shake the thought out of my head. "It must be the jet lag. Either that or I think I did see a ghost."

"Come again?"

"Do you remember Jeremy Johns, that awful New York designer who made our lives miserable during the yacht wedding?"

Kate crossed her arms and narrowed her eyes. "You mean the guy who tried to pull off a hideous South Beach meets South of France design scheme? It rings a bell. Why?"

I shuddered even though it was warm outside. "I could swear I just saw him walking into the hotel."

CHAPTER 2

"Impossible," Richard said as we walked down the wide hallway from our rooms to the elevator. The dark wooden floors and high ceilings of the hall made our voices reverberate, and since his suite was across the hall from mine, he'd heard us heading down to the lobby for tea.

My best friend, and arguably DC's top caterer, looked impeccable, as usual, in black flat-front pants and a freshly pressed blue shirt. Even his dark hair was coifed into neat spikes, making him appear even taller than he was. No one would have guessed that he'd been on planes for nearly two days.

"Why is it impossible that Jeremy Johns would be here?" I asked, stepping around one of the glowing frosted-glass lanterns set along the walls every few feet.

"Jeremy Johns?" Fern asked as he ran to catch up to us, his shoes echoing off the wooden planks. "Why are we talking about that troll?"

Kate jerked a thumb in my direction. "Annabelle thinks she saw him walking from the pool into the lobby."

Fern sucked in air and pressed a hand to his chest. "Why

would Jeremy Johns be here? I thought he vanished without a trace."

"Is that a Hawaiian shirt?" I asked, eying the oversized palm fronds gracing Fern's shirt and stepping into the open elevator. "It's a tropical print." He waved a hand in the air. "Since we're in the tropics."

No surprise that Fern had already dressed to fit the setting. He never missed an opportunity for themed clothing, and I could only imagine what other outfits he had planned for the trip.

Kate pressed the button for the lobby level. "Is it possible Jeremy is part of the FAM trip?"

Fern wrinkled his nose. "I didn't see his name on the list. Unless he's operating under an alias." He nudged Kate. "Maybe he's actually a spy, and the annoying, arrogant-designer persona is all an act."

"Then he's an excellent actor," I said. "I've never been more convinced that someone is a dreadful human being in my life."

The elevator doors opened with a ping, and Richard held them open as we exited. We walked around the elevator bank and down the short flight of stairs into the sunken lobby.

"Wow," Kate whispered.

Wow was right. The wall facing the ocean was floor-to-ceiling glass, and towering square columns ran the length of the expansive open lobby. Multiple groupings of beige upholstered sofas and rattan swivel chairs were topped with orange cushions and clustered around large wooden coffee tables. From the glass wall, we could look out onto the pool, which featured two facing rows of massive stone statues of women carrying shallow bowls on their heads. The statues, ten on each side, rose forty feet in the air and were spaced every ten feet until the pool deck met the sand.

I scanned the lobby and spotted the trip organizer, Carol Ann, sitting with a pair of men and a young blonde. Even though we'd never met, I'd been following her on Instagram since we'd gotten the invitation, and I would have known the curly brown hair and wide blue eyes anywhere.

She spotted us and clapped her hands. "You're here!" Her accent gave away the fact that she was born and bred in Atlanta, as did her perfectly accessorized pink Lily Pulitzer dress and full makeup.

"It's so nice to meet you," I said as she rushed up to us. "I'm Annabelle Archer and this is Kate . . ."

She ignored my outstretched hand and pulled me into a hug. "I know who you are. After this trip we're all going to be like family, so we might as well start off that way, right?"

She moved from me to Kate as Richard raised an eyebrow. He was not one for instant intimacy. We'd been best friends for over five years, and I could count the times we'd hugged on one hand and have fingers to spare.

"Richard Gerard from Richard Gerard Cater—" Richard began before he was crushed into a hug.

Carol Ann released Richard, then appraised Fern's tropical print shirt and brown hair pulled up in a man bun. "You must be . . ."

Fern gave her a wink and pulled her hand to his lips for a kiss. "Fern, darling. Just Fern."

Carol Ann blushed then waved for us to follow her as she walked back across the lobby. "How were your flights? You aren't too jet-lagged are you? It's such an ordeal to get here, but isn't it worth it?"

"She's certainly bubbly," Kate said so only I could hear her.

"I don't think she flew in today," I said. "Since she put together this trip, I'm sure she arrived a couple of days ago."

Carol Ann stopped when we reached the two men and one blond woman I'd seen her sitting with when we arrived. The two men stood and turned.

"You know Cliff and Ted from *Insider Weddings* magazine, don't you?" Carol Ann asked.

I held out a hand. "We've talked on the phone and emailed but never met."

The man with close-cropped brown hair and a tan smiled at me as he shook my hand. "I'm Cliff, the art director. Of course I remember talking with you about your Rose Garden wedding."

The other man's bright-blue eyes widened with recognition. He was equally as tan as his partner but with lighter hair that he wore swept across his forehead. "The Rose Garden wedding was one of our favorites."

"We were very fortunate with that one," I said, taking Ted's hand. "It's not every day you get to do a wedding at the White House."

Fern shook both men's hands. "I did the hair for the Rose Garden wedding."

I could hear Richard sigh next to me. "The one wedding you didn't use me on is the one that's famous."

"You know I couldn't bring an outside caterer into the White House," I whispered to him. "And we've had famous weddings before."

"I don't mean weddings famous for the dead-body count."

I elbowed him. The last thing I wanted was for our colleagues on this trip to find out about our penchant for solving murders at our weddings.

"And this is Dahlia, my right-hand woman. For the past year, at least." Carol gestured to the petite blonde who stood up to greet us, tucking a strand of her stick-straight hair behind her ear. Luckily for Richard, she wasn't a hugger like her boss. "My intern, Kelly, is also with us, but she's still recovering from jet lag in her room."

"Were your flights good?" Dahlia asked, her voice betraying the same soft Southern drawl as Carol Ann's.

I nodded. "Are we the first ones here aside from you?"

Dahlia picked up a Lucite clipboard from her chair and inspected it. "Most folks are here already. A few arrive tonight before dinner, and one or two got delayed and will be here tomorrow. You're the first group to join us for tea."

"Grab a chair, y'all." Carol Ann said, patting the seat next to hers on the beige loveseat.

We all sat—Richard and Kate next to Cliff and Ted, Fern beside Dahlia, and me with Carol Ann. A waiter wearing a black vest with a starched white apron over black pants set white porcelain teacups down in front of us with a small bow. Another waiter came behind him with a three-tiered display of tea sandwiches and miniature pastries.

"Now we're talking." Kate reached for a bite-sized éclair.

I poured myself a cup of tea. "I expected the food to be more . . ."

Carol Ann touched a hand to my arm. "Indonesian? I know what you mean. I was thrown the first day I was served a British high tea. The resort has eight different restaurants, and none serve regular old Indonesian food. But you can try authentic Chinese and Japanese cuisine while you're here. Not to mention Italian, Pan Asian, and French."

I took a bite of a shrimp tea sandwich. It may not have been traditional Indonesian food, but it was delicious. More so since I hadn't eaten a meal in hours.

"How did you find this resort?" I asked Carol Ann once I'd finished my sandwich. "And how did you convince them to host a group of wedding planners?"

Carol Ann laughed. "They were thrilled to do it, honey. One of my clients held her wedding here a couple of years ago. Since then I've been dying to bring more planners over here to show it off. Can you imagine a more fabulous place to hold a wedding?"

I glanced around the glittering lobby and the impeccably dressed staff moving seamlessly from guest to guest. My eyes went to the pool lined with statues and cabanas leading out to the glittering turquoise of the Indian Ocean. It was pretty fabulous.

"And you put together all the activities?" I'd gotten a chance to glance at the schedule for the next few days and had found it filled with meals at all the resort restaurants as well as excursions into the country.

"With the resort staff, of course," Carol Ann said. "Not to mention Dahlia. She's the one who handles all the details. She can keep track of a thousand things at once."

I looked at Dahlia, who was deep in conversation with Fern. I only hoped he wasn't telling her one of his favorite raunchy jokes. They worked well on nervous brides, but I wasn't sure how well they would go over with a sweet Southern blonde who didn't look a day over twenty.

"Hold on to her," I said. "Good assistants are hard to find." I wasn't sure if I always put Kate in that category, but I'd seen enough bad assistants to be glad I had her.

"I don't think she'll leave me." Carol Ann lowered her voice. "I've become like a second mother to her since she started working for me. Her own mother passed away a few years ago. And you'll meet my intern, Kelly, soon. Her mother was also a planner, so she's a natural organizer. Both of my girls are amazing."

Before I could comment, I heard a deep voice call my name. I turned to see Buster and Mack, my go-to floral designers, lumbering toward us through the lobby, collecting stares as they went. I wasn't sure if it was their size that was more striking to people—both men topped six feet and three hundred pounds—or the fact that they each had a goatee, wore black leather with chains, and were bald. On top of it all, Mack had an eyebrow piercing, and Buster wore a pair of black motorcycle goggles on the top of his head.

"I thought you were working with the resort's floral team," Kate said when the men had reached us.

Mack of the dark-red goatee leaned a hand against the back of a chair as he caught his breath. "We're on our way, but we didn't want to walk through the lobby without speaking to you."

"Did you just arrive?" Buster asked, his voice reverberating off the glass and marble in the lobby as he leaned in to give me an air kiss, his dark-brown goatee brushing my cheek.

"Not too long ago," I said. Buster and Mack had flown in on an earlier flight to get a head start training the in-house designers.

Mack gave me a conspiratorial wink. "Aren't the rooms stunning?"

"Do you have your own hot tub?" Kate asked, and Mack nodded with a grin.

"I'm sorry," I said, gesturing to Carol Ann, Dahlia, and the men from *Insider Weddings*. "Do you know Buster and Mack from Lush?"

Carol Ann nodded. "We met when they checked in."

"You can also call us the Mighty Morphin Flower Arrangers," Mack said with a laugh. "All of our biker friends do."

Buster and Mack were members of a Christian biker gang, which meant they drove big Harleys, never cursed, and spent a lot of time praying for our souls. Especially Fern's and Kate's.

Cliff stood and shook their hands. "We only know you by reputation, but your work on the Rose Garden wedding was breathtaking."

"Gorgeous," Ted agreed.

Mack waved away the compliment, but I knew he reveled in it. "Well, when you're in a rose garden, you do roses."

"But a three-sided, ten-foot-high dome of them?" Cliff put a hand to his heart. "And to cover the backs of the chairs with roses, too? It was incredible."

I heard Richard grumbling about being the only one not at the Rose Garden wedding and shot him a look.

"We'd better get going," Buster said. "We have a lot to do before dinner tonight."

"I can't wait to see it," Carol Ann called after them as they hurried out of the lobby. She turned to me and patted my leg. "They sure are something, aren't they?"

"Their work is much less experimental than their personal style," I assured her.

Carol Ann smiled brightly. "Well, it couldn't be wilder, could it?"

Dahlia cleared her throat, and I noticed her face twitch before smiling. "Look who's here."

Carol Ann looked over her shoulder. "Brace yourselves, it's Sasha."

"Sasha?" I asked, recognizing the name but forgetting where she was from.

"Society planner from New York," Dahlia said through her fake smile. "She won't bother with you unless she thinks you can do something for her career."

Kate caught my eye. "Then we should be fine."

"I'm surprised we didn't smell her before we saw her," Carol Ann said, laughing when she saw my expression. "She seems to bathe in Shalimar perfume."

I turned to look at the woman with flaming-red hair and a brightly colored chiffon dress as she wove her way through the lobby. True to Carol Ann's warning, the smell of the heavy perfume reached us before she did.

"Is that a cigarette holder in her hand?" Richard asked.

Carol Ann gasped. "She can't smoke in here."

"It's worse," Kate said. "She's vaping."

Sasha reached us and took a deep drag on her long white cigarette holder but no smoke emerged. "We're finally here."

"We?" Dahlia asked, glancing at her clipboard.

"Didn't I mention that I was bringing my new associate?" Sasha's voice was raspy and revealed the fact that she'd probably smoked real cigarettes for years before switching to electric ones. She turned and beckoned to someone.

"Is that . . .?" Fern said, his voice dying on his lips.

Richard shook his head. "Impossible."

"You keep using that word," Kate said to him.

I watched the man in the mango-colored shirt stride toward us. I would recognize that sneer anywhere. "It's Jeremy Johns all right."

CHAPTER 3

"Of course I'm positive it was him," I said into my cell phone as I stepped into my suite, slipping off my black flats and leaving them in the marble foyer. "If you remember, Jeremy Johns has a distinctive personality."

"I remember him and his personality," Detective Mike Reese said on the other end of the phone. "I'm just shocked he turned up halfway around the world at the same resort as you."

I padded into the bedroom in my bare feet and flopped back on the bed. The white duvet puffed up around me as I sank into the pillow top mattress. I let out a sigh of pleasure. It felt heavenly to lie down after hours sitting in an economy class plane seat and wonderful to hear the detective's deep voice. Even though I'd technically added an international plan to my cell service to keep in touch with our brides, my first phone call had been to Mike.

"Annabelle? Are you still there?"

"I'm here. I just laid down on the bed for a moment."

"I wish I was there with you."

I felt myself blush even though I was alone in the room. DC police detective Mike Reese and I had been involved in what Kate claimed was the slowest-moving relationship she'd ever witnessed. I couldn't deny that it had taken a bit longer than usual for us to reach the point where we were actually dating. It hadn't been clear to me at first that the detective liked me, and it had taken him a while to actually ask me out. On top of that, as a wedding planner and detective, we both had erratic schedules, so making and keeping dates had been tricky at times. But we'd finally gotten our acts together and had been officially seeing each other for a couple of months. I wasn't sure if we were ready to go away together, even if I had been allowed to bring a guest on the FAM trip. We hadn't even slept over at each other's apartments yet. Not that it wouldn't be nice to share my suite with the tall, dark, and handsome detective.

"Bali is beautiful, but you would not have wanted to be on that fifteen-hour leg of the flight from New York to Taipei," I said.

He laughed. "Probably not. But I still miss you."

"I miss you," I told him. And I did. The detective's dark, wavy hair and hazel eyes that deepened to green when he looked at me made my knees go weak. And after seeing him without a shirt, I was positive he was not a cop with a doughnut habit. No one could have muscles like that and eat Krispy Kremes on a regular basis. I tried to put his physique out of my mind, but even hearing his deep voice on the phone made my heart beat a bit faster. "I'll be home in a week."

"It seems like a long way to go for a week."

"Maybe," I said, "but it's a great opportunity for us to get to know some of the biggest names in the wedding business."

"Like Jeremy Johns?"

I rolled onto my stomach and sat up on my elbows. "Ugh. Don't remind me."

"Tell me again how he managed to score himself an invite on such an exclusive trip. I thought his reputation was ruined after the stunts he pulled during your yacht wedding."

"You would think so, right? I know his name is mud in Washington, but maybe not everyone in New York got the memo. He seems to have sweet-talked his way into assisting one of the planners there." I sat up and looked at the clock on the bedside table. I had half an hour before I needed to be dressed and downstairs for the welcome dinner.

"Was he surprised to see you?"

"You could say that." I thought back to the disgraced designer's face when he'd recognized me then had spotted Kate, Richard, and Fern. His eyes had grown wide, and the color had drained from his face, although his fake smile had never wavered. "He pretended not to know us, and I had to kick Richard in the shin to keep him from saying something."

"Why not tell everyone what you know about the guy?" Reese asked.

I pushed myself off the bed and switched my cell phone to my other ear. "Because then I'd have to tell everyone the details surrounding his bad behavior, and I'd rather not have everyone on this trip calling me the wedding planner of death."

"People don't really call you that, do they?" He sounded like he was trying not to laugh.

I stepped into the walk-in closet and ran my hand along the dresses I'd hung up earlier. "Not to my face, but I know people find it strange that Kate and I have wound up in the middle of so many murder investigations."

"Lucky for me that you have such bad luck or we'd never have met."

I couldn't stop myself from grinning as I plucked a peacock-blue cocktail dress from the rack. "True. That's one happy by-product of my clients getting killed."

"And you're sure this Jeremy Johns character isn't dangerous?" Reese asked, always the cop.

"I'm pretty sure." I walked out of the closet and draped the dress across the bed. "He's more of a weasel than a threat."

"Is that Annabelle?" I heard a voice that wasn't Mike's in the background.

I sat on the edge of the bed and started pulling off my pants with one hand. "Who was that? Where are you?"

"I'm at your building. You did ask me to water your ficus tree, remember?"

"Is that Leatrice?" I unbuttoned my shirt and dropped it on the bed then walked into the bathroom and pulled the white terry cloth bathrobe from the hook next to the shower. I glanced out the far glass wall as I slipped on the bathrobe and felt grateful that the tall palm trees blocked people at the pool from having a clear view into my suite.

Reese sighed. "She wants to talk to you."

"I kind of need to get ready—"

"Thank heavens, Annabelle." Leatrice's voice sounded out of breath. "I've been so worried."

"I've only been gone two days, Leatrice. And I'm fine. I'm staying at a very nice resort, so you don't have anything to worry about." My elderly downstairs neighbor had taken an active interest in me since I'd moved in to my Georgetown apartment building six years ago, adding meddling in my personal life to her list of hobbies, which included watching crime TV, listening to her police scanner, and wearing eccentric clothes. She was like a matchmaker, neurotic mother, and head of the neighborhood watch all rolled into one pint-sized, wrinkly package.

Leatrice gave a half snort, half laugh. "Luxury resorts are exactly where they look for people to kidnap and sell into white slavery."

I felt my eyebrows pop up. "You think someone's going to sell me into white slavery?"

"You and Kate," she said. "You're both young and pretty. You're the perfect candidates."

"Have you been watching late-night TV again?"

"*Law & Order*. And you know those shows are based on true stories."

I heard a knock on my door and walked to the foyer as I tied the belt on my bathrobe. "What have we said about you watching true crime shows?"

Leatrice muttered some protests and explanations on the other end of the phone as I opened the door. Richard stood in the hallway wearing a perfectly tailored and pressed tan suit with a hot-pink shirt underneath. His eyes widened when he saw me still in a bathrobe. I waved him inside the room.

"We need to be downstairs in fifteen minutes," Richard whispered as he tapped his Gucci watch. "Why are you not dressed yet?"

I pushed the mute button on my phone and held it away from my ear. "I was telling Reese I'd arrived safely, and then Leatrice got on the line."

"Leatrice?" He gestured for me to hand him the phone. "I need to check on Hermes."

I passed the phone to him. "I still can't believe you let Leatrice watch your dog. I thought you were terrified she'd end up dressing him in weird sweaters and funny hats."

"Oh, I'm sure she'll dress him up in an array of God-awful costumes, but I didn't have a choice. P.J. had to go out of town for a conference. The only other people I'd trust are on this trip with me, so Leatrice was my last resort."

"Don't let her hear that," I said. "She'd be crushed to find out she isn't one of your best friends."

Richard unmuted the phone. "Leatrice? It's Richard. Yes, we're fine. Annabelle's fine." He paused and gave me a funny look. "Of course I'll make sure she doesn't get kidnapped by international sex traffickers. It's at the top of my list."

I shook my head and walked toward the bathroom where I'd already set my makeup out on the marble counter. I could hear Richard assuring Leatrice as I pulled the elastic tie out of my hair and flipped it over. I didn't have time to wash and dry my hair, but I could freshen it up. I groped along the counter for my travel-sized baby powder and shook some into the back of my hair. I ran my hands vigorously through my hair and flipped it back up. I shook a bit more powder into my hairline then brushed it out. My previously limp auburn hair fluffed out around my shoulders. *Much better*, I thought. You'd never know that it hadn't been washed in nearly forty-eight hours.

Richard walked into the open bathroom and rolled his eyes. I could hear Leatrice talking away on the other end of the line.

"How's Butterscotch, I mean Hermes?" I asked, catching myself as Richard narrowed his eyes at me. The little Yorkie had originally been called Butterscotch, but Richard had renamed him Hermes, claiming that the name better fit his personality. I had a feeling it was a matter of the name better fitting Richard's personality, but I would never dare say so.

Fine, Richard mouthed, then he inhaled sharply. "What do you mean you're out of treats already? It's only been two days. I don't care how much of a good boy he is. If he keeps eating treats at this rate, he'll gain ten pounds by the time I get home. I don't want to have to put Mr. Chubbs on a diet."

I swirled translucent powder over my face. "Did you just call your dog Mr. Chubbs?"

He ignored me. "And no junk food, Leatrice. I mean it. It's taken months for me to get him on a healthy eating regimen."

I shook my head and leaned close to the mirror to apply my eyeliner.

"For you." Richard held out the phone. "The hot detective."

"I don't know who's weirder about that dog, Leatrice or Richard," Reese said once I'd taken the phone.

I laughed. "Hopefully watching Hermes will take her mind off worrying about me being sold into a sex-trafficking ring."

"Hopefully." Reese chuckled. "But in all seriousness, Annabelle, you don't have the best track record of staying out of trouble. Promise me you'll be careful."

"I promise. I plan to stay far away from Jeremy Johns." I

lowered my voice so Richard couldn't hear me in the other room. "I'll be back before you know it."

"Good." His voice dropped even lower. "We can pick up where we left off."

I felt my face flush as I remembered where we'd left off on our last date. I turned around and jumped. "Richard!"

"Well, that's not usually the name I like women to call out," Reese said.

I put a hand to my racing heart. "Not you. Richard snuck up on me." I shot Richard a look then noticed the somber expression on his face. "What?"

Richard held out a folded piece of paper. "Someone just slipped this under your door."

"Is everything okay?" Reese asked.

I read what was written in the note. "Not really."

CHAPTER 4

"That Jeremy has a lot of nerve to write that to you," Kate said as we got in a golf cart under the portico off the hotel lobby. Even though the welcome dinner was in the garden near the hotel entrance, it was a long way to walk in heels and dresses.

I slid into the back seat next to Kate and pulled my flowing silk cocktail dress down closer to my knees. I noticed that Kate didn't bother with her formfitting navy-blue dress, and it rode up to mid thigh. Not that I hadn't seen plenty of Kate's legs before, since she didn't own a skirt that went past her knees.

"We don't know it was Jeremy, do we?" Fern asked, turning around from his seat in the front next to the driver and touching a hand to his hair, which was now pulled into a low ponytail.

"Who else could it be?" Richard asked as the golf cart lurched forward, and he clutched the low metal armrest next to his seat in the very back.

I shrugged as we chugged away from the hotel entrance and up the curved driveway. "It was rather cryptic. And it wasn't signed."

Richard threw up his hands in exasperation then grabbed for the armrest bar as the golf cart rounded a curve. "'The question is what can you make people believe you have done?'" He used air quotes as he recited what had been written on the note. "He's clearly making reference to what we know about him and suggesting if we tell people, he'll convince them it didn't happen."

Kate gave a low whistle. "You sure got a lot from that one line."

"Say it is a threat," I began.

"And it is, because we know what kind of lowlife Jeremy Johns is," Richard said. "Plus, vague notes are just the type of passive-aggressive threats he'd make. He's too much of a weasel to actually do anything. Remember how he whispered behind our backs to get us in trouble the last time we worked together."

I gave Richard a look. "Even if it's a threat, what can we do about it? It's not like writing weird notes is grounds for arrest. I'm not even sure what the grounds for arrest are in Bali."

Fern's eyes lit up. "Is this a country that goes in for caning as punishment? If anyone needs a good caning, it's that puffed-up peacock Jeremy Johns."

I noticed our driver's mouth fall open, and I punched Fern in the arm a little harder than I normally would as a joke. "Very funny. No one's going to be caned around here. I'm sure Indonesia has a very progressive criminal justice system."

I wasn't sure about that, but I didn't want my team to insult our Balinese driver with our lack of knowledge. And Bali seemed too groovy to go in for something like caning.

Fern rubbed his arm. "You're no fun."

Our golf cart swung up to a paved entrance where other people in cocktail dresses stood clustered in groups. "The garden," our driver said pulling to a stop.

We thanked him as we got out, and I smoothed the front of my dress once I was standing.

"Who do we know?" Kate whispered to me.

"Aside from Jeremy?" I indicated the blond man with the perma-sneer huddled next to Sasha, who'd changed into another wildly colored dress that reached the floor.

"Clearly aside from him," Richard said. "Although I might want to talk to him about his note later."

I put a hand on his arm. "Let it go. The best thing we can do with an egomaniac like that is ignore him."

"The best thing we could do is find the bar," Fern said.

"Now you're talking." Kate linked her arm through Fern's and headed into the crowd.

"We could get our seating assignment." I nodded to a massive wooden table in the center of the space that had been covered from end to end with a bed of greenery and flowers. Squares of yellow blooms were surrounded by green, giving the tabletop a checkerboard appearance. White cards with names written in swirling calligraphy sat in rows on top of the flowers. This design had Buster's and Mack's names written all over it. As a matter of fact, they'd done this look in pinks and purples for a client of mine only the year before.

Richard leaned over the table to read the names, plucking his card from a patch of green. "They've named the tables instead of numbering them. I'm sitting at the Lovebirds table."

"Great," I muttered. Naming tables had been a trend I'd loved when it came onto the scene a few years ago, but having guests wander aimlessly around ballrooms in search of names of Portuguese villages or types of orchids had changed my thinking on the matter. At least with numbers you had some sense of where you were headed.

A woman with a blond pixie cut and cat-eye glasses approached us. "Can I help you find your names?"

"I think we're good." I smiled at her. "Are you with the resort?"

"I'm with the planner. I'm Kelly." She extended her hand.

"That's right." I shook her hand, remembering the missing intern. "Annabelle Archer with Wedding Belles. Carol Ann mentioned you earlier. How's your jet lag?"

Her cheeks flushed. "Much better." She scanned the names on the bed of flowers and handed me my card. "I've read your name so often on the roster, I feel like I know you already." She gave me a grin and winked at me from behind one cat-eye lens as she turned to help another guest.

I looked down at my card, twisting to face Richard. "I'm at Lovebirds, too."

Richard spared me a smile. "Well, that's a relief. At least one sensible person to talk to."

"What table are y'all at?" A petite woman with dark hair pulled into a high bun asked as she sidled up between Richard and me.

I held up my card for her to see, and she made a pouty face. If I had to guess, I'd put the woman at over forty years old despite her tight green minidress. She wore nude heels that still didn't bring her to my shoulder and bright-pink lipstick that would make her easy to find in low light.

"I'm Dina." She beckoned for a woman with blond, wavy hair that fell to her shoulders to join us. "Veronica and I are at Sweetheart."

"This is Richard, and I'm Annabelle." I held out my hand. "We're from DC."

Richard shook their hands. "Richard Gerard with Richard Gerard Catering."

I gave him an apologetic look. I'd forgotten how much he despised casual introductions. Richard never introduced himself without giving his full name and company.

"I'm from New Orleans," Veronica said. "And Dina here is from Texas."

I noticed that Veronica wore a simpler and less-revealing floral print dress, even though she appeared to be a few years younger than Dina.

"You don't work together?" I asked, as a waiter paused in front of us with a tray of pale-orange cocktails in wide-rimmed martini glasses.

Veronica took two cocktails from the tray and handed one to

her friend. "We're both wedding planners, but we live about two hundred miles apart."

Dina sipped at her drink. "We see each other at FAM trips like this and each year at the Inspire conference."

I nodded as I took a drink from the waiter. I'd heard of Inspire before. It was the most illustrious event for wedding professionals and was known for world-class speakers and top-notch swag. Word on the street was that you'd return from Inspire with tons of motivation and a suitcase filled with gifts.

"How many years have we roomed together at Inspire?" Veronica asked Dina.

Dina held up her fingers while she downed half of her cocktail. "At least five. Our first one was the one in the Cayman Islands."

"That's right." Veronica nudged her and giggled. "The wild one."

"Have you been to Inspire?" Dina asked us. "I don't remember seeing you two there."

"Not yet," I said with a smile. "It's on my list for next year." That was a bit of a lie. I had about fifteen weddings on my list for next year. I didn't know how I would fit a conference into the middle of a hectic wedding season no matter how good the swag.

Dina grasped my free hand. "You *must* come. It's the best time you'll ever have."

Veronica nodded, her smile bright. "It's the only time we can really cut loose if you know what I mean."

Richard raised an eyebrow at me.

Veronica produced her phone. "What are you on Instagram?"

I thought for a moment. "Wedding Belles with an 'e' at the end of bell. All one word."

She typed it in with her thumbs and nodded. "Nice feed. You have a pretty good following, too."

I knew Richard was rolling his eyes even though I wasn't looking at him. He despised the rise of social media and declared it all 'smoke and mirrors.' He wasn't wrong, as there were plenty of wedding planners with huge followings on Instagram who couldn't book or plan a wedding to save their lives.

"We found the drinks," Kate said as she and Fern walked up to us, each holding two martini glasses.

"This is my assistant, Kate, and our friend and hairstylist, Fern." I gestured toward the two women we'd just met. "Dina is a wedding planner from Texas, and Veronica is a planner from New Orleans. They met at Inspire."

"That's funny," Kate said, taking a drink out of one glass and then the other. "We just met a pair of planners from LA who go to Inspire every year together but don't work with each other."

Dina's eyes darted around the crowd. "Kristina and Brett? Where are they?"

Fern waved a martini glass in the direction of the garden entrance, and some liquid sloshed out of the glass. "I think they went to find their seats." He took a long drink. "Those two are a hoot and a half."

"We see them at Inspire every year," Veronica said, then leaned in and lowered her voice just enough to sound conspiratorial. "Brett used to have his own celebrity reality show."

"And Kristina is working on filming a TV special about her celebrity holiday parties," Kate said. "But they're both cool. You'd never know they were from LA."

"Should we find our seats as well?" Richard asked.

I could tell he was getting bored of all the talk of reality TV and celebrities. Not to mention, a little jealous. Richard's biggest complaint about working in DC was our lack of decent celebrities. Sure, some of our clients controlled the free world, but no one could pick them out of a lineup. And they weren't glamorous and photogenic like actors.

Lately Richard had become upset by the number of his clients getting embroiled in political scandal. I knew he was nervous that if conversation turned to famous clients, someone might discover that his past two big-name clients had been indicted for fraud and perjury. One of them was even arrested during a party Richard catered, with photos of the man being dragged out holding one of Richard's signature lamb satay skewers splashed all over the internet. Richard had taken to his bed for three days afterward.

"I'm at the Honeymooner table." Kate held up her seating card. "Anyone else?"

We all shook our heads as we walked toward the entrance to the garden, and Kate shrugged. "That's all right. I bet I'll meet some fun people."

Fern made a face as he looked at his card. "I'm at Sweetheart."

"Us, too," Dina said, pointing to herself and Veronica. "It must be the party table."

Fern raised one of his cocktails. "Cheers to that."

Richard fell back to walk beside me. "These cocktails are so strong that every table will be a party table."

I set my partially full glass on a nearby high-top table as we passed. Richard was right. One more of those deceptively sweet drinks and I'd be on the floor.

We walked down a set of wide stone stairs, and I stopped at the bottom. An expansive green lawn stretched out in front of us with four long tables arranged to look like a giant X extending from end to end. Runners made from greenery and lush white flowers ran down the length of each table, and a collection of towering green-and-white arrangements that resembled Balinese temples stood in the center of the X. Massive illuminated pillars stood along the sides of the lawn, giving light to the tables, while waiters in beige vests and traditional white Balinese hats were lined up behind them.

"Whoa," I said. "Buster and Mack really went all out."

Richard tapped a finger to his chin. "I'd love to get those hats for my waiters to wear."

"You want your DC waiters to wear caps with gold Balinese embroidery on the front?" I asked.

Richard sniffed. "We are an international city, Annabelle."

"Then why do the women wear nothing but black dresses?" I saw Buster and Mack hurrying across the lawn toward us and waved at them.

"I'm so sorry," Mack said, clutching my arm as he reached me.

"Sorry for what?" I looked from his worried expression to Buster's pinched one.

"We meant to move the seating around but we couldn't," Buster said.

I felt a nervous flutter in my stomach. "What's wrong with the seating?"

"Nothing," Mack said. "As long as you and Richard don't mind sitting near Jeremy Johns."

Richard turned to me. "This place has room service, right?"

CHAPTER 5

"How is it possible we're seated next to the one person we despise when there are forty other guests?" Richard asked.

I put a finger to my lips as people passed us on the way to the dining tables. "Keep it down. We don't want to make a scene."

Richard turned to Buster and Mack. "How close are we sitting to that slug of a person?"

Mack wrung his hands. "You're across the table from him and Annabelle is one person away."

Buster's voice came out as a low rumble as his eyes flitted to mine then away. "His boss, Sasha, is between you two."

I let out a breath. "At least there's some buffer. And Richard, you've got a table between you two."

"I'd prefer if I had a continent between us." Richard folded his arms across his chest. "You do remember how he treated us when we worked with him, don't you?"

I remembered all too well. He'd been the designer our client had brought down to DC from New York. His ideas had been as awful as his condescending behavior toward anyone he deemed beneath him. And with Jeremy Johns, that meant everyone. He'd been especially dismissive of Richard, no doubt due to the fact that Richard was stylish and confident and had more talent. Sparks had flown, tempers had flared, and in the end Jeremy had thrown us all under the bus. Richard had yet to get over it.

"Listen," I lowered my voice, "I want to make a good impression on the owners of *Insider Weddings*. They're the ones who got us on the list for this trip. Not to mention the lady who organized this trip. Carol Ann puts together FAM trips all over the world, and I'd really like to be included in the next one. So can we please just suck it up and play nice?"

"Fine," Richard grumbled. "I promise not to make a scene."

Mack visibly relaxed. "I did try to move the cards, but the little blond assistant shooed me away and put them back where they were."

I squeezed his hand. "It's okay. I know how irritating it is when guests move your seating arrangement, so I don't blame her for stopping you. But thanks for trying."

Buster put a thick arm around my shoulders. "You're the reason we're here, Annabelle. Next time we'll just make sure we don't get caught switching the name cards."

I laughed. It was hard to imagine the two massive leather-clad men doing anything incognito.

"Come on." I motioned to Richard with my head. "Let's find our seats."

Mack pointed out which of the long tables was Lovebirds, and we walked across the lawn, me on my toes so my heels wouldn't sink into the grass. I bent low to read the place cards in the low light.

"I need a flashlight," I said, bending over one of the modern white chairs.

"Here I am," Richard called from the other side of the table.

I squinted at a name. "And this is me."

A man with a closely cropped dark beard smiled up at me

from the chair next to mine. "G'day. It looks like we're dinner mates."

I couldn't help noticing what bright blue eyes he had. I pulled out my chair and sat down next to him. "I'm Annabelle. From Washington, DC."

"Alan. From Australia." He held out a hand. "Can you believe this setup?"

"It's pretty amazing." I looked down at the long menu card resting on top of the pearl-beaded dinner plate. A sprig of fresh rice fronds was wrapped in a green ribbon and draped across the menu card.

Alan picked up his menu card. "It looks like there are seven or eight courses."

My mouth dropped open as I inspected my own menu card. The traditional Indonesian food sounded delicious, but eight courses was a long time to sit near Jeremy Johns. Not that I'd seen him yet.

"Have you ever eaten pickled snake fruit?" Alan whispered to me.

"I'm okay with it as long as it isn't pickled snake," I said.

He laughed. "Don't be so sure. I haven't read the entire menu yet."

"How on earth do they expect us to read these in the dark?" The loud voice behind me made me jump. I didn't need to turn around to know it was Sasha. Her perfume preceded her. Plus, no one else in the group was as loud or from Long Island.

I patted the seat next to me with some reluctance. "You're next to me."

"Amy, right?" she asked as she took her seat beside me, her flowing dress ballooning out around her.

"Actually it's Annabelle." I put my napkin over my mouth so I could breath through the cloud of heavy perfume lingering over her.

"Close enough," she said with a dismissive wave.

Alan raised an eyebrow at me and made a face. I pressed my fingers to my mouth to keep from laughing.

"Where is my assistant?" Sasha asked to no one in particular, craning her neck to scan the tables.

"Has he worked for you for long?" I asked, knowing very well that he couldn't have, but wanting to discover more information about how Jeremy Johns had landed on his feet and on Sasha's payroll.

Sasha gave a curt shake of her head. "Only a couple of months. He came to New York after working in Paris."

"Really?" I said. I couldn't help but be impressed by the scope of Jeremy's deception. If he'd been in Paris, it had only been because he'd been on the run from the last client he'd bilked out of money. "How did you manage to snag him?"

"He wanted to work with *me*." She smiled and swept her unnaturally bright-red hair off her shoulder. "He says he only works with the best."

I nodded. That sounded like Jeremy Johns. Pander to the egos of older women and watch them fawn all over you.

Alan nudged me and made a gagging motion with his hands. "I think you and I need a drink. Want to hit the bar?"

I stood up. "Excuse us, won't you?" I said to Sasha as Jeremy approached the table.

I ran a few steps to catch up to Alan. "Just in the nick of time."

Alan looked over his shoulder. "Is that the crawler she was talking about?"

"Crawler?" I asked, wondering if I'd heard correctly.

He laughed. "Australian for someone trying to get in good with someone else."

I glanced back at Sasha and Jeremy. It was clear she was scolding him for being late as he took the seat next to her. I couldn't help smiling at the strained expression on his face. "Then that's a perfect word for Jeremy."

"If you ask me, he looks like a wanker." Alan grabbed my hand.

"If we have to sit next to those two, we're going to need some serious cocktails."

I didn't know if it was the Australian accent or the fact that he'd already saved me from Sasha and Jeremy, but this guy was fast becoming my favorite person on the trip.

We crossed the lawn to the bar set up in the corner. A man and woman already stood leaning against the illuminated Lucite bar.

The woman had fluffy, blond hair and wore a long multicolored-striped dress with spaghetti straps. The man was equally blond with short hair and wore black pants and a black shirt open at the throat. Both were tanned and talked like they knew each other well.

"You two look like you need a drink," the woman said with a big smile.

"You could say that," Alan said. "We're sitting next to a scary lady."

The man in black looked over our shoulders. "Which one?"

I hesitated to say her name for fear that these two knew her or, worse yet, were friends with her.

"Sasha," Alan said. "The New Yorker with the purple hair."

The blonde rolled her eyes. "She's one of the reasons I'm glad we live in LA."

I snapped my fingers. "I think you met my assistant, Kate, during cocktails."

The man grinned. "We loved her. Where is she sitting?"

I looked back at the giant X-shaped table but couldn't see Kate. "At Sweetheart, wherever that may be."

"I'm Kristina and this is Brett." The blonde handed me a martini glass filled with a clear liquid as the bartender passed it to her. "And you need to try this drink."

I took the drink and sipped it. It was strong but not overly sweet.

"Isn't is good?" Kristina asked. "None of that fruity nonsense. I like a cocktail with clean, simple flavors."

Brett passed an identical drink to Alan then took two more from the bartender and raised his glass in the air. "To new friends and avoiding scary people."

We all clinked our glasses then drank.

"I cannot believe you left me there," Richard said as he hurried up to us. "With *them*."

I made introductions. Richard managed to shake hands all around.

Brett handed Richard a drink. "We're toasting to avoiding scary people."

"Cheers to that." Richard tossed back the cocktail in one gulp.

"We didn't mean to leave you," I explained.

Richard set the empty martini glass on the top of the bar. "I think the word you're looking for is 'abandon.'"

Before I could mollify Richard, Dina and Veronica walked up. Veronica wobbled the last few steps, and I wondered how many colorful cocktails she'd already enjoyed.

"It looks like the party's at the bar," Dina said.

Kristina held up two fingers to the bartender. "Two more, please." She turned back to the two women. "You must try this drink."

"It's simple and clean," Brett said. "Just the way Kristina likes it."

Kristina swatted at him. "Are you making fun of my cocktail?"

Brett took the two filled martini glasses from the bartender and passed them to Richard who handed them to Dina and Veronica. "Never. You know I think you have exquisite taste."

Veronica splashed some of the drink onto her hand as she tried to hold it steady. "Between the fruity drinks during cocktail hour and the pregaming we did at the bar with Carol Ann and her team, I'm feeling a little dizzy."

"Don't forget we haven't eaten in hours," Dina said. "Once you get food in you, you'll feel better."

"What's everyone doing over here?" Carol Ann ran up in her very high heels. "The first course is being served."

"Sorry, sweetie," Alan said, putting his empty glass back on the bar. "We'll go sit down right away."

Veronica and Dina teetered off, clutching each other with one hand and holding their drinks with the other.

"Talk to you later." Kristina gave me a small wave as she and Brett headed across the lawn.

Alan linked arms with Richard and me, pulling us toward our table. "Let's go eat some snake fruit."

I took my seat next to Sasha again.

"Where were you?" she asked, giving me the once-over.

I noticed that Jeremy Johns wasn't sitting on the other side of her anymore. "What happened to your assistant?"

"I had him go get me a pashmina." Sasha flipped her hair back. "No one told me we'd be sitting outside for hours."

I wondered what part of "dinner in the garden" had confused her, but I kept my mouth shut. I found the air to be balmy and the slight breeze to be pleasant. Before I could think of a new topic of conversation, I heard a scream from across the lawn. I twisted around in my chair and spotted Dina standing and shrieking.

"What's going on?" Alan asked.

A murmur passed through the crowd as people began standing and hurrying over to Dina. I pushed back from the table. "No idea, but she seems hysterical."

Alan rose next to me. "I'll go see what's happening."

As he left the table, Richard came around the table and slid into his chair. "I don't have a good feeling about this, Annabelle."

I rubbed my arms briskly despite the fact that the air wasn't cold. "Maybe she saw a snake. They have snakes in Bali, right?"

I watched several men wearing black jackets and hotel name badges rush across the lawn. Carol Ann stood next to Dina, her arms wrapped around her. My snake story seemed less and less likely.

Alan returned to the table and stood behind Richard. I looked up at his face and noticed that his mouth was set in a grim line.

"Is everything okay?" I asked, even though I knew in my gut it wasn't.

He shook his head. "That girl Veronica collapsed and isn't breathing."

"But we just saw her at the bar," I said. "She looked fine."

"Well, they're doing CPR on her," Alan said.

Kate hurried up to us with Fern close on her heels. "Can you believe this?"

Fern's eyes were wide. "I saw it happen. She did not look good before she went down."

Richard reached out and grasped my hand. Goosebumps pricked my arms as my stomach clenched. I knew Richard was thinking the same thing I was. *Not again.*

CHAPTER 6

K ate lowered her sunglasses over her eyes as we rode the golf cart up the curved driveway the next morning. "What kind of taskmasters serve breakfast at eight o'clock?"

"Eight in the morning is not an unreasonable time for breakfast," I said, hanging onto the side of the cart as we swung up to the entrance to another of the resort's buildings. Like the section of the resort that housed our guest suites, this building was expansive and open with wide marble steps leading to a massive lobby with more neutral-colored furniture and blond wood. "What's unreasonable is our bride Natalie calling me at four in the morning."

Kate shook her head. "Neurotic Natalie called you at four a.m.?"

I flipped my ponytail off my shoulder. "To be fair, it was four p.m. her time, and I didn't expect our brides to memorize the time difference."

"It's exactly twelve hours different. All you need to do is switch the a.m. to p.m. in your head or vice versa," Kate said. "Easy peasy."

I didn't remind her that I was the one who'd drilled that into her head before we left. "Well, it wasn't easy peasy to give Natalie a coherent answer about flower girl sashes at four in the morning, I can tell you that much."

"Is she still going on about those?" Kate asked. "Did you tell her she should go with the blue and move on?"

"You know I did. Let's hope hearing it for the tenth time will do the trick." I stifled a yawn. "Eight a.m. really wouldn't be so early if I hadn't had the wake-up call four hours earlier."

"It's still early if you were up late being questioned by the police." Richard hopped out of the back of the golf cart once it had come to a stop and held out a hand to me as I stepped down.

I took his hand and used the other hand to keep my knee-length purple sheath dress from riding up. I took a deep breath, enjoying the fresh morning air and breathing in the scent of frangipani blossoms from a nearby arrangement.

"Not to mention jet-lagged," Fern moaned. "My body thinks it's eight o'clock at night not eight in the morning."

Kate patted him on the shoulder. "Join the club."

"Do we take naps in the club?" Fern asked. "I could really go for a nap."

"Listen," I said as we walked up the steps. "If we can power through today, our bodies should start to reset themselves to Bali time."

"I'm not sure we need to power through today so much as survive it," Kate said as she leaned on Fern's arm, her high-heel mules clacking on the cream-colored marble tiles. "You do remember that one of our colleagues died last night?"

I'd tried to push the mental image out of my mind, but the sight of the blond planner sprawled on the lawn, her eyes lifeless and her lips purple, was not one I'd forget anytime soon. "Of course I do." I lowered my voice as we walked through the lobby on our way to the cafe. "But the police don't know what caused her to die. It could have been accidental. Some people get fatal blood clots after long flights."

Richard eyed me. "You're reaching."

I looked up at the large, star-shaped skylight in the ceiling as we passed underneath. A spiraling yellow-and-white art installation hung from above, and natural light poured in from the wooden slats lining the glass. "I refuse to believe that she was murdered."

Kate looked at me over her sunglasses. "Because that would make us the angels of death?"

I glanced at a woman sitting in a royal-blue armchair and hoped she hadn't heard what Kate said. "No, and I don't want anyone on the trip to find out anything about our past run-ins with dead bodies either."

"You don't need to worry about us spilling the beans, Annabelle." Fern pantomimed locking his lips and throwing away the key.

"But we aren't the only people who know." Richard led the way as we walked down the twisting staircase to the promenade level.

I thought about Jeremy Johns and my heart sank. He wouldn't hesitate for a second to tell everyone within shouting distance about the deaths that had taken place when we'd worked together.

We reached the promenade level and crossed to the entrance to a glass-walled dining room. A coffee bar was set up outside the tall doors with two Balinese baristas in white jackets standing behind a pair of shiny cappuccino machines. I could almost taste the rich coffee on my tongue as I breathed in the aroma.

"Thank heavens," Kate said when she saw the chalkboard propped next to the bar listing the coffee drinks available. "I don't think I've ever needed coffee as much in my life."

Fern leaned against the coffee bar and batted his eyelashes at the baristas. "A double espresso, and give it wings."

"Can you order me a cappuccino?" I asked Richard as I spotted Alan standing with Brett and Kristina.

"There you are," Alan said, giving me a quick hug when I joined the group. "We wondered if you and your mates had slept late. We're all knackered after last night."

I shook my head. "It wasn't easy rousing everyone, but we're here."

"Dina hasn't come down yet," Kristina said. She wore a black halter top and white jeans, and her pale hair fell loose around her shoulders. Somehow she managed to make a simple outfit look very hip. I figured it must be a trick people from LA knew, because Brett wore a plain green T-shirt and khaki shorts and still looked like he stepped out of the pages of GQ.

"Do you think she will?" Brett asked.

"Maybe she's at the gym." Kristina took a sip of her coffee. "She was always at the gym early during Inspire. That's another reason I didn't hang out with her."

Kate shuddered. "I don't know if I'd make breakfast if my friend had died. And I definitely wouldn't hit the gym."

"She didn't just drop dead," Alan said. "She was murdered."

"Murdered?" I stared at him, glad that some of his words weren't Australian slang. "Who said she was murdered?"

"I heard the police talking to hotel security last night after they questioned me. They think it looks suspicious."

"They said something about poison."

I shook my head as if trying to dismiss the idea. "But they haven't had time to run a tox report or test food for poison."

Alan raised an eyebrow at me. "Maybe her external symptoms point to poison? That's why they took all her plates and glassware to be tested. To find out how it got into her system."

"Are you okay?" Kristina asked, putting a hand on my bare arm. "You look a little pale."

"Did you know Veronica well?" Brett asked.

"No," I said. "It's just shocking to hear she might have been murdered. She seemed nice."

Kristina looked at Brett. "She was pretty nice. We knew her from Inspire. She and Dina always came together."

I glanced at the growing group of people around me and noticed a line extending from the coffee bar. "It seems like most of the people here know each other from Inspire."

Alan ran a hand along his short beard. "I haven't been, but I hear it's stellar."

"I think everyone here either knows Carol Ann through Inspire or knows Cliff and Ted from *Insider Weddings* magazine," Brett said.

A waiter in a black Nehru jacket passed by and invited us into the glassed dining room for breakfast. I turned and spotted Richard heading for me with two cappuccino cups.

"Just in time," I said, taking one of the white porcelain cups with a heart pattern swirled into the white foam on top.

We followed the crowd into the dining room. Several large, round tables were topped with bright arrangements of red-and-yellow Gerbera daisies. Each place setting had a round woven placemat made of shimmering gold fabric topped with a colorful menu card.

I set my cappuccino down at an empty table. Richard and Alan took the seats next to me with Kate and Fern sitting on the other side of Alan. Kristina and Brett were across from me, and Buster and Mack rushed up to claim the last two seats next to Richard.

"Did you two sleep in?" I asked, leaning over Richard so Mack could hear me.

Mack sighed. "I wish. We were up early to work with the hotel design team."

"We can't manage to sleep in even when we're at a luxury resort," Buster said. "Not that I could sleep much after last night."

I noticed the dark circles under both men's eyes. "It was pretty upsetting."

A waiter set a trio of juices in short cylindrical glasses in front of me followed by a glass plate of artistically cut fruit. My stomach growled at the sight of the food, reminding me that I had barely taken a bite of food since the day before. I'd certainly been too upset to eat dinner after Veronica had collapsed.

"It was the first time we've been at the scene of a murder," Mack said. "Every time your clients have been killed, we've been somewhere else."

I waved a hand to shush him. "Let's not share that fact, okay?"

"We were there when the diamonds were stolen," Buster added, his voice sounding even louder in the glass-walled room. "But never for the murders."

Mack's face brightened. "That jewelry heist was pretty exciting, though."

I tried not to groan out loud. So much for keeping things under wraps.

"Don't worry," Alan said. "Everyone already knows that you've had a lot of clients cark it."

I nearly choked on my cappuccino as I took a sip. I lowered the cup slowly to the saucer. "What?"

"Get killed," Alan said.

"I think Crocodile Dundee is making up these words," Richard whispered to me.

"Not all of the people killed were clients," Kate corrected Alan, waving a wedge of melon on the end of her fork. "Some of them we didn't even know."

"And not all of the dead clients were my clients," Richard said. "But Fern knew them all."

Fern leaned over Kate and winked at Alan. "Guilty."

I closed my eyes and wondered if I could slip underneath the table and disappear. I steadied my breath and opened my eyes to look at Alan. "Who told you this?"

He slipped a thin silver flask out of his pants pocket and pointed it across the table. "Kristina and Brett mentioned it this morning. Anyone else up for making our coffees Irish this morning?"

Kate's face brightened. "I think you and I are going to be best friends."

I tried to ignore the giggling as both Fern and Kate passed their coffee cups across to Alan. "Kristina and Brett," I repeated.

Kristina looked up when she heard her name. "Yes?"

"Alan said you told him something about me this morning." I tried to keep my voice light, but I could hear the quaver in it.

"That you guys had been involved in murder cases before?" She nodded. "It sounded pretty cool to me."

"Who told you?" I asked.

"Someone I'd never met before." She twisted in her chair to scan the room. "He was with the lady with really red hair."

"Blond hair?" Richard asked. "Fussy clothes? Upturned nose?"

Kristina thought for a second while Brett answered for her. "Definitely."

"I knew it," I said under my breath. "That fink Jeremy is spreading rumors about us."

"He has a lot of nerve," Richard said. "Not much taste, but a lot of nerve."

I speared a berry with my fork. "Especially since he's probably still wanted for grand larceny."

Richard stroked his chin. "Does Indonesia have an extradition agreement with the U.S.?"

"I don't know, but I don't think getting him arrested and extradited is our best move."

Kate peered over Alan. "There's more than one way to skin a rat."

Alan grimaced. "You Americans have the oddest expressions."

"Yes, darling, but that's not one of them," Fern said.

"He's one to talk," Richard said under his breath. "I'll bet half of the Australian words he uses aren't even real."

I elbowed him. "Behave. He's perfectly nice."

He glanced at Alan and shrugged. "If you ask me, he's a little much."

I stared pointedly at Richard's purple polka dot pocket square and matching ascot.

He inhaled sharply and put a hand to the puffed-up knot of silk around his neck. "I'll have you know this is couture."

I stared at him, unblinking.

"Fine." He rolled his eyes. "I'll be nice."

"So no extradition for Jeremy," Fern said. "What do you suggest, Annabelle?"

"I think it's time we had a little chat with our old friend," I said.

CHAPTER 7

"Since when has talking to Jeremy ever produced results?" Richard asked after he'd finished his plate of crab cake eggs Benedict topped with black truffle hollandaise sauce, dabbing the corner of his mouth with his napkin.

"There's a first time for everything," I said, although I remembered all too well our unsuccessful attempts to talk with the prima donna designer when we'd been forced to work with him on a wedding. I took a bite of the smoked salmon and caviar scrambled eggs wrapped in puff pastry. The salty and savory flavors were a delicious combination, and I closed my eyes for a moment as I swallowed.

"This trip is going to be murder on my figure," Fern said as he eyed the petite filet mignon and baked egg in brioche in front of him. His gaze fell on the french toast topped with strawberries and mascarpone cheese that Kate was eating. "I suppose it could be worse."

"Hey," she said. "After last night I need some comfort carbs."

"When we talked to Jeremy before, we didn't have leverage," I explained. "Now we do."

Since Alan had gone back to the coffee bar for another latte, I could talk freely to my friends about Jeremy. As much as I liked Alan, I didn't want him to know all our dirty laundry.

"So we're going to threaten to tell everyone that he's a thief unless he stops spreading rumors about us?" Kate asked before tossing back a shot of green juice.

"Pretty much." I looked around the room where the group sat eating at round tables. Conversation had been subdued and quiet, a somber hum without any laughter. A reflection of last night's tragedy, I was sure. I spotted Sasha but didn't see Jeremy next to her. Instead there was an empty chair, and I wondered if he'd been sent to fetch another pashmina.

"Be careful," Mack warned, leaning across Richard. "You remember what Buster and I told you about working with him in New York. He won't hesitate to lie, cheat, or steal to come out ahead. And we have the ruined business to prove it."

I did remember my friends' tale of Jeremy destroying their reputation when they worked in New York City. I studied the two burly men with their goatees, black leather ensembles, and hearts of gold. I'd never seen them angrier than when they'd found out their former nemesis was working on a wedding with us in DC. Mack had nearly burst a blood vessel, and Buster had muttered some words that sounded suspiciously blue.

"Why are you two not more upset that Jeremy is here?" I asked.

"We've added yoga and meditation to our prayer meetings," Mack explained while Buster nodded. "It's helped us release past anger and anxiety."

I didn't know if I wanted to imagine the two massive men doing yoga. "Your Christian biker prayer meetings?"

"One of our members is becoming certified as a yoga teacher," Buster said, sopping up strawberries and cream with a forkful of french toast. "So he's practicing on us."

"Heaven preserve us," Richard muttered.

The idea of a room of Harley-riding men wearing yoga pants

was almost more than I could take. I pressed my fingers to my lips to keep from laughing.

"You should come to one of our meetings, Annabelle. It helps with the wedding stress." Mack gave Richard a pointed look. "You, too."

"Wild horses couldn't drag me there," Richard said.

"Don't take it personally," I told Mack. "Yoga isn't really Richard's thing."

It wasn't really mine, either, but at least I'd never stomped out of a class like Richard had when a teacher had suggested his root chakra was backed up.

"Well, even if you aren't angry at Jeremy anymore, you still know him better than anyone else here," I told Buster and Mack. "How do you suggest we handle him?"

Buster muttered something under his breath, and Mack placed a hand on his thick forearm. "Breathe out anger, breathe in love."

Richard rolled his eyes. "If you ask me, the only way to stop someone like Jeremy is to fight fire with fire."

"Did you say set him on fire?" Fern asked. "Because I think that would really do the trick."

Kate leaned over. "We're setting someone on fire?"

Alan paused as he returned to the table holding his latte and looked from Fern to Kate to me.

"Joking," I said with a wave. "We were only joking."

He sat down and shook his head. "I've never understood American humor."

I gave my friends a look that told them to cool it. I sat back to let the waiter take my plate and noticed Jeremy had returned to the room and seemed to be headed for the coffee bar. I pushed back my chair and dropped my napkin on the table. "I'll be right back."

I walked quickly across the room and through the glass doors, a smile plastered on my face. I came up behind Jeremy as he ordered a vanilla latte. "I hear you've been a busy little bee, buzzing in everyone's ears."

He jumped when he saw me, then his lips curled into his customary sneer. "Well, if it isn't the ringleader herself."

"I thought it might be good for us to talk in person before the rumors get out of hand." I reminded myself not to let him bait me as I felt my breath quicken.

He gave a dismissive shrug. "I haven't said anything that isn't true."

I clenched and unclenched my fists. "Maybe, but don't you think you're leaving out the part of the story where you stole thousands of dollars and ran out on the client?"

Jeremy's eyes darted around him. "I deserved that money."

"Not for that hideous wedding design you inflicted on us," Richard said as he walked up. "*You* should have paid everyone who had the misfortune of seeing it."

Jeremy sucked in his breath as he turned on Richard. "You take that back."

Richard crossed his arms over his chest and looked Jeremy up and down. "Never. You're a talentless hack who preys on people who are too naive to know better."

Jeremy's face turned purple, and he stamped his foot. "You can't talk to me like this."

"Why not?" Richard glanced around us. "You don't have a rich client under your spell to threaten us with."

"I'll tell everyone about your clients getting killed," Jeremy said, his voice a hiss.

Before I could protest, Richard shrugged it off. "Haven't you already done that? Anyway, if you share your information, then we'll be inclined to share ours. With the police. I'm sure the authorities would be very interested to know that an American wanted for grand larceny is vacationing on their island. I hear the Indonesian prisons are lovely this time of year."

Jeremy spluttered. "You're bluffing. You wouldn't make a scene like that."

Richard laughed. "I love making scenes. Ask Annabelle."

I nodded. "It's his specialty."

Richard brushed some imaginary lint off Jeremy's shoulder. "So why don't you run off before someone drops a house on you."

I smiled sweetly at him. "We'd hate for something bad to happen to you."

Jeremy looked from Richard to me and back again. "You can't threaten me and get away with it." He leveled a finger at us. "You'll regret this."

"Is everything okay out here?" Carol Ann asked as she walked out of the dining room with her assistant, Dahlia, and her intern, Kelly, in tow.

Jeremy flounced off without another word.

"It's fine," I told her. "Just a disagreement."

Richard snapped his fingers. "And we forgot to thank him for that sweet note he left you."

"That's right. It completely slipped my mind," I said.

"Did you know him from before?" Dahlia asked, tucking a strand of blond hair behind her ear.

"Unfortunately," Richard said.

I elbowed him. "We worked together once."

"You know, he wasn't even on the guest list," Carol Ann said. "Sasha insisted on bringing him. I thought he was new to the business. I'd never heard the name Jeremy Jenkins."

"Jeremy Jenkins?" Richard and I said in unison.

"Isn't that his name?" Carol Ann glanced at Dahlia.

Dahlia looked at Kelly before she bobbed her head up and down. "That's the name Sasha gave us. Jeremy Jenkins."

"Who's Jeremy Jenkins?" Kate asked as she and Fern joined us.

"You know," I said. "*Jeremy.*"

Fern scratched his head. "Maybe it's the jet lag, but that doesn't sound right."

"Excuse me," Carol Ann said as a pair of black-clad Balinese men approached us. "That's hotel security. They may have more information for me about Veronica."

I watched her and her assistants huddle off to the side with the men, their heads together in hushed conversation.

"So what's with Jeremy Johns going by a fake name?" Kate asked after she placed an order for an espresso.

"I'm sure he's trying to fly under the radar," I said. "As far as I know there's still a warrant out for his arrest in DC."

"I think an alias is exciting," Fern said. "Maybe I should have an alias."

Richard tapped his foot on the marble floor. "That would be the cherry on top."

"But I already have a pretty fabulous name." Fern drummed two fingers on his chin. "If I had an alias it would need to be something on the opposite end of the spectrum. Like Joe."

Richard put a hand over his eyes. "Oh, for the love of everything holy."

Kelly hurried over to the coffee bar. "Do you have any water back there?"

"Is everything okay?" I asked when I saw her worried expression.

"It's for Carol Ann." She motioned to her boss who stood with her head hanging between her knees, her brown hair nearly skimming the floor as Dahlia rubbed her back. "She's not handling the news about Veronica very well."

"What news?" Kate asked.

Kelly bit the edge of her lip. "They found traces of antifreeze on the inside of her mouth and the rim of one of her glasses."

Fern sucked in his breath. "Antifreeze? How awful."

"So soon?" I asked. "Are they sure?"

She nodded as the barista handed her a glass of water. "It looks like it. Apparently antifreeze has fluorescein in it that can be detected using a black light. The police here had bartenders spiking drinks with antifreeze a few years ago, so they knew to test for it." She gave us a weak, apologetic smile. "I should get this to Carol Ann."

"I do *not* like this, Annabelle," Richard said, loosening his ascot with one hand.

"I know poison freaks you out, but she wasn't poisoned by food, and you weren't the caterer. It's an entirely different situation." Richard had once been a murder suspect in a poisoning case, and he'd never gotten over the fear of being falsely arrested. I'd never been sure if it was prison itself or having to wear an orange jumpsuit that had been his greater fear.

"But don't you remember?" He fanned himself with a paper cocktail napkin from the coffee bar. "We were drinking with Veronica right before she went back to her table."

"That's right," Fern said. "She and Dina both tried Kristina's cocktail."

Richard's chin dropped open as a look of realization crossed his face. "And I handed the drinks to them." His voice dropped to a whisper. "I might have delivered the murder weapon."

I caught him as he slumped against me, and we both sank to the floor.

CHAPTER 8

"You almost broke my ankle, you know," I said to Richard as we clambered into a black van.

"My apologies," Richard said, his voice dripping with insincerity. "The next time I'll aim for someone with more muscle tone."

I slid over to the window seat in the front row and rubbed my calf. "How about next time you don't swoon like the heroine of some Regency romance novel?"

Richard inhaled sharply as he took the middle seat next to me. "I did not swoon. I was merely overcome with emotion when I realized that we are, once again, embroiled in a murder investigation."

"Embroiled seems like a strong word," Kate said, taking the seat directly behind me. "It's not like we knew the victim well. They can hardly think any of us had a motive."

"Enough murder talk," Fern said as he leaned in the sliding door of the van. "The reason we're sneaking away from the resort is so we can get a break from all of that."

After they'd pulled Richard off of me and hoisted me off the floor, Fern had made a beeline for the hotel's concierge and arranged for a driver to take us sightseeing in Bali. He'd said he couldn't handle a day spent talking Richard off the ledge. If it was one thing Fern despised, it was someone being a bigger drama queen than him. At Fern's instruction, we'd all put on bathing suits under our clothes, even though he refused to tell us our destination. Richard's white linen blazer and purple polka dot ascot had been replaced by a black button-down shirt and perfectly creased tan pants.

Mack thumped Fern on the shoulder, causing the hairstylist's knees to buckle. "I, for one, think it's a brilliant idea. Buster and I have been so busy training the hotel staff that we haven't seen anything but the floral design room."

"Are you sure we won't get in trouble with Carol Ann for going off schedule?" Buster asked as Mack scooted his way to the back seat.

Fern massaged his shoulder as he sat next to Kate. "Carol Ann's assistants gave her a Xanax to calm her down. That Georgia peach will be out for hours. Besides, we'll be back in time for the dinner at Sky Bar."

"And tonight's dinner has very little floral decor," Mack reminded Buster. "So as long as we're back by midafternoon, we'll be fine."

The van lurched forward and we drove up the curved drive-way, pausing at the massive walls made out of giant bronze rosettes that framed the resort entrance before making a right onto the two-lane road. Tall knotty trees stretched their branches overhead and were interspersed with palm trees along the street. The flag of Indonesia, a band of red on top of a band of white, was tied to trees on both sides, and the fabric flapped in the breeze. A stream of people riding motor scooters passed us going in the opposite direction, some riding single file and some in pairs.

"Look at all the bikers," Buster said.

Mack peered out the window. "Who knew that Bali had a biker culture?"

I didn't point out that these small motorbikes were a far cry from their massive black-and-chrome Harleys and seemed to be more practical than stylish with thin wheels and little embossed leather. Not to mention the fact that if Buster and Mack tried to ride a Balinese scooter, I felt sure they would crush it.

"Where are we headed?" I asked the driver, a Balinese man named Wayan, meaning firstborn, with neatly parted black hair and a ready smile.

"Temple and waterfall," he said, catching my eye in the rearview mirror. "Up north."

I pointed to a stone structure with a thatched roof along the side of the road that was flanked by two ornamental statues. "Is that a temple?"

He shrugged. "House temple."

Kate leaned forward. "What's a house temple?"

"Families have private temples on their property," Wayan explained. "Very common."

"That's interesting." I pointed to an ornate orange building set back from the road, fronted by a stone statue of a dancing god. The god's face looked like an exaggerated mask with bulging eyes, large pointed teeth, and a curled beard. I couldn't imagine having something like that in front of my apartment building in George-town. Then again, I had Leatrice to ward off evil spirits and unwanted solicitors.

"You've got to admit the belt is fabulous," Fern said. The statue did have a wide stone belt that extended past its feet, covered with flowers and ornate scrolling patterns and centered with what appeared to be a monster-face belt buckle.

"That's one way to describe it," Richard said.

We drove down an open stretch of road with swaths of rice fields on both sides, the golden-green plants bending and swaying under their weight. Wayan pointed out the women in cone-shaped straw hats gathering the stalks of rice in bundles and pounding them in wooden troughs. "Old-fashioned way."

"I thought rice was grown on the sides of hills," Richard said as he flipped through his Bali guidebook. "Isn't Bali famous for the terraced rice paddies?"

Wayan nodded. "More north."

Richard's phone trilled. He fished it out of his leather bag, glanced at the screen, and sighed. "Yes, Leatrice?" He listened for a moment, then held the phone out to me. "She wants to talk to you."

I put the phone to me ear, my stomach clenching in anticipation of bad news. Had a pipe burst? It was winter in DC, after all, and our building was old. "What's up, Leatrice?"

"I wanted to run this by you first, in case Richard got his nose bent out of shape," Leatrice said, Hermes yipping happily in the background.

I twisted around so Richard couldn't see my face. "What are you up to?"

"Nothing," Leatrice said. "But what do you think Richard would say about a pet psychic?"

I glanced back at Richard, who had his arms crossed and his eyes narrowed. "Nothing I could repeat in mixed company."

"Oh." Her voice sounded deflated.

"Are you planning on hiring one or becoming one?" I asked.

"Aren't you a stitch?" Leatrice giggled. "Hiring one, of course. Although pet psychic might not be a bad job for me, come to think of it. I've always had a bit of the second sight."

Just what I needed—Leatrice to add communing with the dead and having psychic visions to her array of nuttiness.

I lowered my voice. "This is a bad idea. Why did it even occur to you?"

"I think Hermes is a very intuitive dog. He seems to have instincts about people when we go to the park. I thought if I brought in a proper psychic, Hermes could tell me things about some of the people I'm keeping an eye on."

"Who are you keeping an eye on?" I asked, trying to make my voice stern. "Are you illegally surveilling people again?"

"It isn't illegal to observe people," Leatrice said. "Especially when you're ninety percent sure they're Russian moles."

I put a hand over my eyes. "Oh, good lord."

"Hermes agrees with me. "The dog yipped again in the background. "And I'm sure he could tell me more with the proper channeling."

"Absolutely not," I whispered, scooting further down the seat away from Richard so he couldn't overhear me scold my neighbor. "Richard will have a fit if he finds out."

"Fine." Leatrice sighed loudly. "But don't blame me when it turns out the Russians have a sleeper cell embedded in Georgetown."

"I promise," I said. "Now I have to go."

I clicked off and handed the phone back to Richard.

"Well?" he asked.

"She called to tell me she let herself into my apartment to let all the faucets drip." I purposely looked out the window to avoid his penetrating gaze. "It's going to be below freezing in DC this week."

He made a noise in the back of his throat that told me he only partially believed me.

"Lucky us to be here instead of there," Fern said. "It's always warm near the equator."

I lay my head back on the headrest and closed my eyes. The exhaustion of the trip, coupled with the stress of the past few hours and Leatrice's latest crazy idea, seemed to be catching up with me. Not to mention the lulling motion of the van. When I woke, we were pulling over on the side of a road overgrown with thick foliage.

"We're stopping at a coffee plantation," Richard said as he scooted toward the door to the van and slid it open.

"Perfect," I said, following him. "I could use something to wake me up."

A large stone sign reading "Cantik Agriculture Luwak Coffee" sat near the edge of the road with a pair of open-air wooden huts nearby. Wayan waved us to a path with a bamboo door leading into the jungle.

I followed Richard, pausing to wait for the rest of the gang when I reached the entrance. Buster and Mack were right behind me, but Fern stood by the van as Kate tied a black-and-teal paisley sarong around his waist. This was not a surprise as Fern prided himself in dressing to the theme of any occasion. I'd been shocked he hadn't worn a full Balinese headdress on the plane.

"What are you doing?" I called back to them.

"Getting in the Bali spirit," Fern said, taking tiny steps toward me in the snugly wrapped sarong that nearly reached his feet.

"I hope you can walk faster than that," I said. "It looks like there's a long path into the jungle."

Fern picked up the pace, jogging without moving anything above his knees.

Richard turned around and his eyes rolled heavenward. "You look like a geisha girl being chased."

Fern stuck out his tongue as he caught up with us. "You're just jealous that you don't have an authentic batik sarong."

"Where did you get it?" I asked. "We've barely been here twenty-four hours, and this is the first time we've left the hotel."

"I took a walk on the beach this morning. Once you get away from the hotel zone, there are quite a few people selling things. Sarongs, massages, jewelry."

Not surprising since our resort was in a tourist area with quite a few luxurious hotels.

"Are you all coming?" Mack asked from a few feet inside the jungle. "Coffee awaits."

We walked down the pebbled path into the dense jungle, a bamboo railing guiding us through the twists and turns. As we emerged from the path, a pair of metal cages, each topped with a tin roof, sat off to one side. Several black-haired animals reminiscent of foxes lay curled up inside.

"What are those?" Kate asked Wayan who waited for us by the cages.

"Civet cats," Wayan said. "They make the luwak coffee."

Kate tilted her head. "What's luwak coffee?"

Richard scanned a page of his Bali guide. "Poop coffee."

"I beg your pardon?" I said.

"The palm civets eat the coffee beans but can't digest the stone of the coffee berry, so they poop them out and that's what's used to make luwak coffee," Richard read from his book. "It's supposed to be the best coffee in the world."

Kate put a hand on the cage. "Poor civets."

Fern made a face. "They're not the ones drinking the poo, darling."

"Still," Mack said, "do you think we could break them out?"

I patted them both on the back. "You know how much I love to do illegal things, but why don't we try not to get arrested on our second day here?"

Wayan led us away from the cages and toward a wooden hut with open sides overlooking more dense green jungle. A series of long polished-teakwood tables with benches on each side filled the huts, each table topped with a large yellow laminated place mat with descriptions of the various coffees for sale.

"Being arrested for liberating cats would be better than being arrested for murder," Kate said, swinging one leg over a bench.

I sat across from her. "For the last time, we aren't going to be arrested for our colleague's murder."

"Murder?" Wayan cocked his head to one side. "Why are you talking about murder?"

"One of the women with us on this trip was poisoned last night at our hotel," Kate explained.

Wayan shook his head. "This is a bad thing. Bali didn't have crime before visitors."

"None?" Fern asked, taking tiny sideways steps to sit down on the bench.

"Balinese have a philosophy," Wayan said. "What happens to you, happens to me."

"I like that," Buster said, pushing his black motorcycle goggles up further on his bald head.

"We are a small island, so we are all neighbors," Wayan continued. "If our neighbor suffers, we suffer. We only have crime from people who visit."

"So there's no way our colleague could have been killed by someone from Bali?" Richard asked.

Wayan's dark eyes widened, and he shook his head vigorously.

"We didn't suspect the staff anyway," I reassured him as a wooden tray lined with twelve glass cups was placed in front of us. The glasses were each filled with a different drink and ranged in color from milky brown to deep mocha to garnet red. The server took the glasses off the tray and arranged them on the yellow place mat so they matched up with the coffee descriptions. He explained each variety, leaving us to taste them at our leisure. Luwak coffee, or poop coffee, wasn't included in the sampling, much to our relief. Even if it were the best coffee in the world, the thought of the caged civets would have spoiled the experience.

"Then who do we suspect?" Richard asked me once Wayan had walked away to chat with the staff. "We know it wasn't one of us."

"Motive and opportunity." I raised the cup of coconut coffee to my lips and took a small sip, savoring the rich flavor. "Once we figure out those two things, we'll know who did it."

Mack nudged Kate. "I guess we know who's dating the cop, don't we?"

I noticed Richard purse his lips. He wasn't crazy about me dating Reese, although to be fair, he'd never warmed to any of the men I'd dated. Kate insisted that he would be less jealous if I included him in the relationship, but I barely had enough time to date Reese, much less Richard and Reese together.

"Whoever killed her must have really hated her." Fern lifted a glass of dark-brown coffee, his pinky finger outstretched. "Antifreeze is an awful way to do away with someone."

Mack shuddered. "I'm glad I was nowhere near when it happened."

Fern took a sip then replaced the glass and lifted the one next to it. "To be honest, I didn't know she was poisoned. She just dropped dead like she'd had a heart attack."

I paused with the cup of vanilla coffee halfway to my lips, the sweet scent giving me pause. I wasn't an expert on poisons, but I felt pretty sure it would take a lot of antifreeze to make someone drop dead like that. Fern was right. Whoever killed Veronica must have held more than a grudge against her. They must have despised her. I wondered what the wedding planner had done to warrant such hatred.

CHAPTER 9

"T hat was the perfect day," Fern said as he shimmied out of the van, shopping bags filled with packs of fragrant coffee swinging from his shoulders.

We stood under the covered portico in front of our resort as the bellmen greeted us with wide smiles. I glanced into the open lobby with its towering glass walls overlooking the pool and leading toward the beach. I heard the quiet clinking of china cups from the few guests having afternoon tea at low marble-topped tables, but otherwise the resort felt serene. I breathed in and smelled the faint saltwater of the ocean, feeling a sense of relief that I didn't spot any of our fellow attendees lounging on the sleek beige furniture enjoying savory tea sandwiches and fruit-filled pastries. I didn't relish dealing with the fallout from Jeremy's gossip.

Kate glanced at her phone. "And it's only midafternoon. We still have plenty of time before dinner."

"That's our cue to go start working on the floral design," Buster said, nudging Mack.

Mack threw his arms around Fern, who stumbled back a few steps. "Thanks for putting together the field trip."

Fern righted himself and smoothed his sarong. "Don't mention it. I always say that shopping can cure just about any woe."

"Leave it to you to find a retail opportunity in the middle of the jungle," Richard said, but I knew from his own coffee-filled shopping bags that he'd enjoyed the outing.

Buster and Mack headed off in the direction of the hotel's design studio,while the rest of us walked up the marble steps into the lobby.

"It wasn't all shopping," I said. "The waterfall and temple were beautiful."

"Speaking of those," Kate said, "Bali needs more elevators."

I knew what she meant. My legs still ached from climbing the hundreds of stairs down to get a good view of the impressive Tegenungan waterfall as water poured over the high rock cliffs to the pool below. Only Kate had been brave enough to swim in the cold water at the bottom of the fifty-foot waterfall, getting close enough to the rushing water cascading over the falls to have her hair soaked by the spray, but we'd all splashed around in the rocky shallows before trudging up the hundreds of steps to our van. But not before taking a photo of Fern next to the rustic wooden sign that instructed tourists "don't worry, be sexy" followed by a smaller sign underneath reading "but not naked."

"My new motto," Fern had exclaimed when he spotted the sign.

We'd groaned when our driver had explained that the famous Gunung Kawi Hindu temple complex, with shrines carved into the stone cliffs, could only be reached by a series of at least a dozen long staircases down into a valley. We'd walked down hundreds of stairs and past massive trees, their knotty branches stretching wide and draped with vines that reached the ground and swayed in the breeze. We'd crossed stone bridges over a rushing stream to get a better look at the ornate pyramid designs set into the stone, the ground above them verdant and topped with palm trees.

I rubbed my thighs, remembering the wide temple complex we'd finally reached— a stone platform with a series of thatched-roof temple structures, some small and some large, gilded on the inside and guarded by stone gods lightly covered by moss. The two sides of the towering stone entrance to the temple complex were designed like a pair of carved stone staircases moving from low steps on the outside to the twenty-foot peak in the middle, but with a space between them in the center wide enough for us to walk through. "But it was worth it."

"Maybe so," Kate admitted, "but I'm ready to lie on the beach for a while."

I pointed to her platform sneakers. "Maybe next time skip the heels."

"These aren't heels," she said, switching them out for a pair of flip-flops in her beach bag. "They're designed to sculpt my calves."

"Can I borrow them later?" Fern said, hitching his shopping bags higher on his shoulders as he shuffled toward the beach with baby steps.

We walked through the lobby and out the glass doors to the pool deck, then made our way past Dahlia and Kelly, lying with eyes closed in a cabana, to a row of cream-colored lounge chairs with matching umbrellas. I put on my sunglasses to shield my eyes from the bright sunlight as I stretched out on one of the lounge chairs. Kate did the same next to me while Richard unfurled a beige hotel towel, smoothing it on the chair before he sat down.

"I suppose it's time to lose the sarong," Fern said with a frown as he unwound the fabric from his waist, revealing a banana yellow Speedo, and laid down next to Richard.

Richard gaped at Fern's eye-watering bathing suit as he tied the laces of his black board shorts into a prim bow.

Kate picked up a leather-bound menu on the glass-topped table between our two loungers. "I'm ready for a drink."

"You must try the Elderflower Crush," a woman wearing a

wide-brimmed straw hat two lounge chairs away from us said. "It's one of the mixologist's specialties."

I waved at her. "Thanks. You sound like you know the ropes around here."

She sat up and held her hat on her head with one hand. "My husband and I got here a few days ago." She pointed to a man standing at the edge of the ocean. "We're on our honeymoon."

"You've got to be kidding me," Kate said low so only I could hear her. "Can we not go anywhere without brides stalking us?"

"Should we ask her where she got married?" Fern said as he leaned over the drink menu with Kate.

"Absolutely not," Richard said, his voice a hiss. "Unless you want to spend the next hour listening to every detail about her wedding."

"If she says she used blush sequined linens I may just have to gouge my own eyes out," Kate said.

I coughed loudly so the bride couldn't hear my friends. "Congratulations. Thanks for the cocktail tip."

"No problem. I did a ton of research before we came here." She laughed. "You should have seen all the research I did for our wedding. My wedding planning binder was huge."

"Make it stop, Annabelle," Kate whispered.

Fern nudged her. "Ten bucks says she whips out the binder from her beach bag."

A shadow fell over my legs. "Where did you all run off to after breakfast?"

I looked up as Kristina sat down on the edge of my chair and felt relieved that her arrival had caused the Type A bride to lie back down on her lounger.

Brett dropped his beach bag on the sand next to Kate. "We heard there was some fight with that prissy designer from New York, then you and Richard fainted."

I sat up and slid my sunglasses down my nose. "Hey, you two.

First of all, I did not faint. I merely caught Richard when he fainted on top of me."

"Who's saying I fainted?" Richard asked. "Stumbled. I stumbled, and Annabelle happened to catch my fall."

A waiter passed by and took our drink orders, leaving the leather menu so Kate could ponder what she should have for her second cocktail.

"Did everyone hear about our fight with Jeremy?" I asked.

Kristina waved a hand in the air. "Everyone thinks he deserves to be threatened. He's been a jerk since he arrived."

"They're saying we threatened him?" I groaned. The last thing I needed was to get a reputation as a hot head with all the top wedding planners. Not to mention the editors at *Insider Weddings* magazine.

Richard shrugged. "We did threaten him."

"Only because he threatened us first," I insisted. "He said he'd spread rumors about us. We were merely defending ourselves."

"No one's blaming you, honey," Brett said.

I sank back onto my chair. "This trip is not going like I imagined it would."

"Aside from the murder and the fact that our nemesis is here," Fern said, "it hasn't been so bad."

I noticed the bride's eyebrows disappear beneath her hat at the word "murder." I closed my eyes and leaned my head against the chair cushion, taking a slow breath and trying to calm myself. I could hear the gentle sounds of the ocean as it met the sand, and I focused on that as I told myself that things weren't so bad.

"This should help," Kristina said as an ice cold glass was pressed into my hand.

I opened my eyes to see the rocks glass filled with crushed ice, a pale golden liquid, and mint leaves. I took a sip and let the refreshing sweetness fill my mouth. "Delicious."

"Want to try my Lychee Caipiroska?" Kate held out her glass garnished with a fleshy round lychee fruit.

Brett held up his frothy green concoction. "Cheers to this trip improving."

Richard raised his glass, and I noticed that he'd also ordered an Elderflower Crush. "I'll drink to that."

"I know there's been a murder," Kristina said. "But at least we aren't dealing with some of the scandals we've had at Inspire."

"That sounds juicy. What kind of scandals?" Kate popped the blush-colored lychee in her mouth.

Brett set his cocktail down on the glass side table and began hunting through his beach bag, producing a black tube of expensive sunscreen. "You know how conferences can be. People are out of their element, and the booze is flowing. It's an alternate reality—like being on a cruise ship."

"Are you trying to say that people fool around?" I asked. I'd heard of indiscretions at corporate conferences or conventions, but it had never occurred to me that wedding people would behave the same way as stifled businessmen.

Kristina nodded. "I mean, there have been some genuine romances to come from Inspire, but there are no shortage of hookups either."

Brett squeezed some cream into his palm and spread it on his already-tanned arm. "And since there aren't tons of straight men to choose from, the competition and jealousy can get fierce."

It was true the wedding business wasn't packed with many options for single, straight women to choose from. I should know. I'd been a single wedding planner for years without meeting an eligible bachelor who wasn't either a guest at one of my weddings or in the wedding party. And I had a hard-and-fast rule about not dating groomsmen or relatives of clients, which left a very small pool. Mostly DJs, married photographers, and bandleaders with groupies. Not a great selection. I felt lucky that I'd finally met Detective Reese.

"I never got sucked into that mess." Kristina pointed to a

wedding ring on her finger. "But there are a few people on this trip who did."

"Like who?" Fern nearly fell off his chair trying to lean closer to her.

"This was before my time." Kristina took a bite of the white jicama stick garnish from her cocktail. "But Sasha was rumored to have a long-running affair with a lighting designer from Texas."

Brett snapped his fingers. "That's right. They'd meet up at Inspire conferences and award ceremonies every year. Apparently, they rarely made it out of the room to hear the speakers."

Richard made a face. "Sasha?"

"She was younger and thinner," Kristina said. "But also married."

"Yikes," I said. "That's not good. I feel bad for her husband."

"For a lot of reasons," Richard mumbled.

"What happened?" Kate asked. "I'm guessing it's not still going on."

Brett dropped the sunscreen back in his bag and picked up his drink. "Didn't she leave her husband for him?"

Kristina gasped. "That's right. I'd forgotten about that part. She left her husband for him, but after all that he didn't marry her."

Fern shook his head. "Men are dogs."

Brett drained the rest of his cocktail and waved for the waiter. "From what I heard, he was the type of man who was only interested in her when she was unavailable. Once she was free, he moved on to someone else."

Even though I found her abrasive and condescending, I couldn't help feeling sorry for Sasha. That must have been a devastating blow. Maybe being burned like that was the reason she was so abrasive in the first place. "Who did he move on to? Someone else in the wedding biz?"

Kristina shook her head. "I don't remember. Someone young and new. But that was a one-time fling that didn't last. Then he stopped coming to conferences. Last I heard, he'd settled down with a woman in Texas who has no connection to events."

Brett inhaled sharply. "I just remembered the name of the young thing he dumped Sasha for."

Kristina slapped a hand over her mouth as she must have remembered as well.

Brett nodded, his eyes wide. "Veronica."

CHAPTER 10

"It can't be a coincidence two women who dated the same man are here," I said, slipping my sheer black bathing suit cover-up over my head and standing up.

Richard tossed back the rest of his drink in one gulp. "And that one of them is dead."

"Hell has no fury like a woman's thorn," Kate said.

Kristina's brow furrowed, and I could see Brett mouthing the expression to himself. It wouldn't take them long to figure out Kate was the queen of malaprops.

"You sure you don't want to walk down the beach with us?" I asked Kate and Fern as Kristina and Brett stood to join us.

Kate lay back on her lounge chair. "I got plenty of exercise on the stairs this morning. I'm going to soak up some sun so people back home will know I went to a tropical island."

Fern raised his unfinished, and second, cocktail to us. "I could never leave a job half done, darling. But be sure to tell the sarong ladies I said hi. The lady who sold me mine was twelve."

Richard's mouth fell open. "She was twelve years old?"

"No, she called herself twelve."

Richard put one hand on his hip. "Her name was twelve?"

Fern sighed. "They have licenses to sell on the beach. Numbered licenses. She was number twelve." He reclined on his lounge chair and slipped oversized black sunglasses over his eyes. "Be careful, though. She's good at haggling."

"We're going to check out the rest of the beach, not shop." I pulled my hair up into a high ponytail.

Brett swung his beach bag over his shoulder. "I'm going to bring my money just in case."

We cleared a cluster of palm trees and headed down the beach, walking four across with Kristina and Brett in the middle. We wound our way through the resort lounge chairs on the sand with open umbrellas, and I recognized some familiar faces from dinner the night before. One woman with a brown topknot glanced up as we passed.

"Don't stop," Brett said out of the corner of his mouth. "That's Cathy from St. Louis. We call her Chatty Cathy."

"If you get sucked into a conversation, you'll never escape," Kristina agreed as she sped up her pace.

I saw a couple I remembered from dinner stretched out on side-by-side lounge chairs holding hands.

"Jacob and Katherine," Brett whispered to me. "Aren't they adorable? Those two actually met at in Inspire and have been together ever since."

I spotted Sasha sitting on a lounge chair, wearing a straw hat so wide it nearly touched Jeremy in the lounger beside her. She had her phone pressed to her ear as she talked loudly to someone about tent permits. I coughed as I inhaled a cacophony of Shalimar, suntan lotion, and salt air.

Jeremy glanced at us and slid his sunglasses down his upturned nose. "Didn't you and your little team run off?"

"We didn't run off," I said, using my fingers to make air quotes. "We went sightseeing."

Jeremy arched an eyebrow like he didn't believe me. "I thought maybe you were trying to escape all the gossip about you and your friends."

Brett and Kristina looked at me, a questioning look on their faces.

"You mean the untrue rumors started by you?" Richard asked.

Jeremy shrugged. "If it isn't true you've had multiple clients drop dead at your weddings, I'll be happy to correct my statements."

"At least we didn't embezzle money like some people," I said, noticing Chatty Cathy look over as our voices rose.

Jeremy's eyes narrowed, then he gave a haughty laugh. "But the Balinese police aren't investigating embezzlement, are they? I'll bet they'd be interested to know that several people on this trip have actually been suspects in a murder investigation before."

I balled my hands into fists, but before I could think of something to say in response, Brett took my elbow and spun me around.

"I thought we were taking a walk," he said, propelling me forward and away from Jeremy.

Kristina linked her arm through Richard's and dragged him with her as he hurled an insult about Jeremy's knockoff Prada flip-flops over his shoulder.

We walked down the hard-packed sand until we'd reached the edge of the water. I looked out into the ocean and saw the waves breaking further out, making the water close to the shore flat and placid. The sea extended out in bands of blue, from a pale turquoise at the sand to teal as the water deepened to indigo where the waves crested. I relaxed my hands and tried to put Jeremy and his threats out of my mind as I took in a breath free of spicy perfume.

"I'm sorry about that," I said to Kristina and Brett.

"I'm just sorry I didn't get to tell him what I thought about his bargain basement spray-on tan," Richard said, clearly still fuming.

"Don't give it a second thought," Kristina said, patting Richard on the shoulder. "Jeremy makes enemies everywhere he goes."

"How do you know everyone?" I asked.

Brett winked at me. "I'm not as young as I look. Plus, almost all the people on this trip are Inspire people. Different cliques but I still know who they are."

Since I was on the end closest to the ocean, I let the water wash up around my feet, feeling pleasantly surprised by the warmth of the water. "And Chatty Cathy is from Inspire?"

Kristina nodded. "She tried to hang with Dina and Veronica more than with us though."

"Which was fine by me," Brett added.

"So whom did Sasha pal around with at Inspire?" Richard asked. "Aside from the guy she had an affair with?"

We crossed from our resort's beach area into what appeared to be a public beach with an open-air restaurant and plastic lounge chairs grouped closely together in tight rows. A thatched hut with a pair of high massage tables sat over to one side, and two bored masseuses sat underneath talking to each other.

Kristina thought for a moment. "Come to think of it, I don't know if she did hang around with a group. And after the affair ended, she never returned to Inspire."

"That's sad," I said.

"She was cheating on her husband for years," Richard reminded me. "Plus, she's the reason Jeremy is here."

I gave myself a mental slap. "Right. Forget I said that." I stepped around a stretch of crushed shells in the sand. "Do you think Sasha could have killed Veronica to get revenge after all these years?"

Brett and Kristina exchanged a glance, and Brett shrugged. "I don't know her well enough to say, but she doesn't seem like the most easygoing person."

"But why wait all this time to take her revenge?" Kristina asked. "And it's not like Veronica stayed with the guy. He married someone else. I'd have an easier time believing Sasha flew out to Texas and killed him."

We passed a row of rust-colored beach umbrellas, and I looked up at the hotel behind them. Sprawling, with chocolate-brown stairs leading up to a large building surrounded by lagoon-like swimming pools, the resort looked luxurious. As we walked further down the sand, members of the hotel staff were setting up a dark wood ceremony structure draped with white fabric in front of three short rows of folding chairs. Four fabric-draped poles marked off four corners of the beach, each topped with a large floral ring reminiscent of a wagon wheel, with white tassels dangling underneath.

"A wedding," Richard said, more like a curse than a statement.

I sped up my pace. "We do seem to have a hard time avoiding brides and weddings on this trip."

"I don't mind weddings," Kristina said. "Of course I don't do them all the time. I do a lot of big galas."

"It would be nice to have the occasional event without a bride," I said. "Their emotional needs can drain you."

Brett walked around one of the standing floral rings, reaching up and tapping one of the tassels. "Try doing a wedding for a celebrity bride. Or, even worse, a reality TV celebrity bride."

Richard made a face. "That's the one saving grace of DC. No reality TV stars."

"Be careful what you wish for," I said, shuddering at the thought of reality TV stars descending on my understated and classic city.

"Annabelle's right," Brett said. "They're the worst. They're not famous, but they think they are, so they want everything for free. And if they don't get their way, they go off on Twitter. It's a nightmare."

Suddenly our brides weren't looking so bad.

"But at least you have recognizable famous people," Richard said. "Our famous people are politicians. Most people couldn't pick them out of a lineup no matter how powerful they are. Plus, they aren't pretty. I wouldn't mind having some pretty people."

I tried not to roll my eyes. "We have pretty brides."

Richard sighed. "But the grooms, Annabelle. What about the grooms? You're not going to stand here and tell me that the Secretary of Commerce or Treasury or whatever was a looker."

Richard was right. I was not. And I wasn't going to defend his bride either. Although the raven-haired actress was one of the so-called pretty people Richard craved, she hadn't been a pleasant client, and I was thrilled to have that wedding in my rearview mirror.

"Should we head back to the hotel?" Kristina asked. "I'm definitely going to need to shower and wash my hair before dinner tonight."

We reversed ourselves, passing the wedding setup again. This time there was a small wooden table under the wedding ceremony structure and more chairs had been added.

"So, just for argument's sake, let's say Sasha didn't kill Veronica," I said. "Who else might have a reason to murder her?"

Richard narrowed his eyes at me. "Why don't we leave that to the police?"

"You heard our driver this morning," I said. "The Balinese don't have crime unless tourists bring it. That means they're not going to know how to get inside the mind of a killer. Which means they probably won't figure out who did it."

Kristina raised an eyebrow. "Someone likes true crime."

Richard crossed his arms over his chest. "Someone thinks she's Columbo just because she's dating a detective."

Kristina's face lit up. "A detective? Is he cute?"

"If you like the dark and smoldering type," Richard said before I could answer.

"We do," Brett said, giving me an appreciative nod.

Kristina nudged me. "Nice going, girl."

I felt a blush creep up my neck. "Back to the murder. Who else on this trip has a motive?"

"What if Sasha herself didn't kill Veronica but brought Jeremy with her as a hit man?" Richard suggested.

I gave Richard a pointed look and lifted my long cover-up as a wave splashed my feet. "I know you hate Jeremy and would love for him to go to prison, but that seems like a bit of a stretch."

"Veronica and Sasha weren't the only people who shared partners at Inspire," Brett said. "There are definitely people who hook up with someone new each time. Long-lasting couples like Jacob and Katherine are rare."

"So did Veronica steal anyone else's boyfriend?" I asked. "You said she hung around with Chatty Cathy. What about her?"

Brett shook his head. "Not that I ever heard about. Cathy didn't have the same luck as some of the other women. Maybe because she would talk you to death before anything could happen."

Kristina snapped her fingers. "Do you remember that big scandal a few years ago? With Dina and Veronica and another woman?"

"A sex scandal?" Richard asked, lowering his voice as he said it, even though there was no one near us. "With three women?"

"It wasn't between the women," Kristina said.

"I think I remember hearing the gossip about it afterward," Brett said. "Didn't one of them have an affair with a slick photographer and end up getting divorced over it?"

"Like Sasha," I said, wondering how many marriages were ruined by business conferences. I'd never known wedding conferences to be hotbeds of infidelity, but clearly I'd been a bit out of the loop.

We reached the public beach and walked up to the tables and chairs set out on the sand. A lone waitress was delivering food to the few customers, and my stomach growled as I watched a guest nibble on a skewer of grilled meat and another twirl noodles onto a fork. Due to Veronica dropping dead last night, I'd yet to try Indonesian noodles or satay, two of the dishes the country was famous for. We wound our way through the tables and into our resort's beach area.

"Did Veronica have the affair?" I asked.

"I don't think so, but to be honest, the details are a bit fuzzy," Kristina said. "You should really ask Dina. She's the only person here aside from Veronica who was involved."

Brett pointed to a figure stretched out on a lounge chair just two away from Kate and Fern. "You can ask her right now. Isn't that Dina?"

I leaned down as we approached the chair. Although her dark hair was fanned out around her shoulders and not in a high bun like it was last night, I recognized the petite woman behind the round tortoiseshell sunglasses. I took a breath to gather my courage. "Hey, Dina."

She didn't respond.

"Is she sleeping?" Kate asked when she spotted us. "She's going to burn like a lobster with that fair skin if she's not careful. She already looks a bit pink."

"How long has she been here?" I asked, noticing the three empty martini glasses on the table beside her chair. A white-and-orange container of Roche-Posay sunscreen peeked out of her beach bag next to her bubble gum-pink Sigg water bottle.

Fern sat up and took off his sunglasses, holding a hand over his eyes to block the sun. "She came out right after you all left for your walk. She said she'd been clearing her head on the treadmill and was ready to drown her sorrows."

"That makes sense," Kristina said. "She was always a bit of a workout fanatic."

Brett pointed to the metal water bottle. "And an Inspire fanatic. That's from the conference the year it was in Playa del Carmen. I think I still have mine somewhere."

Richard pointed to the empty martini glasses. "And a fan of cocktails."

I shook the woman's foot gently, not surprised she'd passed

out after chugging multiple drinks. "Wakey, wakey, Dina. Time to get out of the sun."

Nothing. I felt a cold chill go through me despite the heat.

Brett sat down on the lounge chair next to her, and Dina's hand slid off her waist and flopped down onto Brett's leg. He jumped up and slapped a hand over his mouth.

"What's wrong?" Kristina asked, looking from him to Dina.

He lifted his hand from his mouth and choked out the words. "It's cold. Her hand is cold."

I bent down and gingerly lifted Dina's sunglasses. Her eyes were wide and unblinking underneath. I dropped the glasses back on her face and stood up, looking at the stricken faces around me.

Fern came up and put an arm around my shoulder. "Is she . . .?"

I swallowed hard. "She's dead."

CHAPTER 11

"Is it true?" Carol Ann rushed toward us with Dahlia and Kelly close on her heels.

We'd gathered on the sand a few feet away from the hotel security team surrounding Dina—far enough so we weren't staring at the dead woman's face, but close enough to answer any questions that might arise about how we'd found the body. I'd turned my back on the morbid scene, but I could still hear the hushed conversation, although I didn't understand the Indonesian words the security team exchanged.

A group of other hotel guests, including Chatty Cathy, stood apart from us, watching the activity and whispering about it. I noticed Sasha and Jeremy were no longer at their loungers, and I wondered when they'd slipped inside. I tried to ignore the stares, but I recognized the murmured gossip. Fern's arm remained around my shoulder; it was the only reason I hadn't collapsed onto the ground from shock.

Kristina caught Carol Ann by the arm before she reached the body. "It's true. The security team is securing the scene until the police arrive."

Carol Ann looked wildly around her, her eyes darting from

face to face. "This can't be happening. It just can't. People don't die on wedding planner FAM trips."

"You haven't been on one with us before," Richard said under his breath.

I shot him a look. "Maybe this was an accident, Carol Ann. We don't know it was another murder."

Carol Ann waved a hand in the direction of Dina. "Why would a forty-year-old woman drop dead while lying in the sun?"

I fought the urge to look over my shoulder. Just the thought of Dina's glassy stare and waxy skin made me go cold.

"This is a plot." Carol Ann waved a finger in the air. "Someone is trying to ruin my reputation by wrecking this trip and knocking off all the guests."

Dahlia slipped an arm around her boss's waist as she hurried up behind her. "You've been working too hard, and the stress is getting to you. Why don't we go back up to your room? I'm sure the hotel will keep us posted on the investigation."

Carol Ann put her face in her hands and burst into tears. "I didn't mean what I said. I'm just so upset." She sobbed. "I can't believe Dina is dead."

Brett enveloped her in a hug. "That's okay, doll. We know you didn't mean it. This is devastating to all of us." He looked up at Dahlia. "I can take her upstairs for you."

"I'll go with them," Kelly said, flicking a hand through her short blond hair.

"Thanks," Dahlia said. "I'll be right behind you."

We all watched as Brett and Kelly led Carol Ann away, her shoulders heaving as she cried into his shoulder.

"What did she mean about this being a plot?" Kate asked once Carol Ann was out of earshot.

Dahlia sighed. "This is only our second time bringing planners to a resort, but Carol Ann hopes to make this a division of our business. A profitable one."

Kristina nodded. "So having planners dying definitely doesn't help sell the service to other resorts."

"Not so much." Dahlia pulled her pale hair into a messy ponytail. "But I doubt she's seriously concerned about sabotage. It was the stress talking. Who would benefit from our FAM trip planning not being successful?"

I shrugged. "Are there any other planners trying to do the same thing?"

"Or any planners on this trip who've decided they want to do what you're doing?" Richard asked.

"You'd have to be pretty psychotic to murder people on the off chance of stealing business," Kate said.

Richard cocked an eyebrow. "These are wedding professionals we're talking about."

"We don't even know for sure this was murder," I repeated. Even though it looked bad, I didn't want to jump to conclusions. I also didn't like thinking there was a serial killer on the loose in paradise.

Fern patted my arm. "You keep telling yourself that, sweetie."

"I'd better get back to Carol Ann," Dahlia said. "If you find out anything, can you let us know?"

We assured her we would.

"When do you think we can leave?" Richard asked in a loud voice, casting a glance over his shoulder at the black-clad security officers.

"Soon, I hope." Kate put a hand to her hair. "I still need to get ready for dinner."

"Are we still having a dinner?" Kristina asked. "Last night's was a total bust, and we only made it to the first course before someone dropped dead. Today we haven't even gotten that far and another woman is killed."

"Talk about a subdued beachside barbecue," I said, referencing the dinner's theme. "The dress I had planned for tonight is much too cheery."

Fern's face creased with worry. "I'm not sure what to wear. My embroidered Balinese pants don't exactly go with multiple murders, either."

I felt my phone buzz in my bag, and I pawed through the contents until I found it. I glanced at the name on the screen and pressed the talk button.

"I'm glad you called," I said to Reese as Fern gave me a smug smile, and I took a few steps away from the group.

"Miss me already?" His deep voice sounded slightly flirtatious.

"Yes," I admitted, letting out a shaky breath. "I wish you were here right now."

"What's wrong?" Reese asked, his voice less suggestive.

I paused for a moment as I considered how much to tell the detective. It wasn't like he could rush to my rescue from half a world away, but I knew that telling him everything would make me feel better. Not to mention he might have insights into the situation from his years on the DC police force.

I turned to observe the Balinese police officers that had just arrived and stood huddled around the body. They wore black cargo pants and short-sleeved shirts the color of stone, covered with pockets and patches. Black berets with a shiny gold badge pinned to one side covered their close-cropped hair. Between the hotel security officers and the newly arrived police, all I could see of Dina were her bare legs stretched out on the lounge chair. My eyes fell on her perfectly polished red toenails, and I shuddered. I'm sure she'd gotten a pedicure before the trip, just as Kate and I had. I wondered how much more we had in common with the two victims.

"Annabelle?" His voice snapped me out of my own thoughts.

"I'm sorry." I turned away from the crime scene. "It's a bit of a madhouse here. One of the other wedding planners was killed. Well, we aren't sure she was killed, but we know the first one was."

Silence on the other end of the phone.

"Are you there?"

"Two wedding planners have been killed since I spoke to you yesterday?"

I rubbed a hand over my eyes. "Yes, but I have to say, you seem to be taking this pretty calmly."

"I'm just trying to digest the fact that you only arrived in Bali yesterday and already you're mixed up in a homicide. Correction. Two homicides. To be honest, Annabelle, I'm starting to think that you or one of your friends might actually be a serial killer."

"Very funny," I said.

"Were you anywhere near the victims when it happened?"

I sat down on the edge of a nearby empty lounge chair. "Not at the dinner last night. Veronica was seated at a different table, but I actually discovered that Dina was dead about an hour ago."

He groaned. "You found the body?"

"Well, I wasn't alone. Richard was with me and a couple of planners we met from LA. And the victim was lying on a lounge chair on the beach, so it was pretty public."

"Is there any way I can convince you to get on the next plane back to DC?" he asked.

"I just got here." I looked over my shoulder at my friends who were now being questioned by a Balinese police officer. "Besides, I don't have any connection to the women who were killed, but they were friends so it's clearly not a random thing."

"Or it *is* random and the fact that they're friends is a coincidence. And you do have something in common. Aren't you all wedding planners on the same trip?"

I hated when his arguments made so much sense. "Fair enough."

"Tell me more about the first murder." His voice was all business. "I need more background."

I thought back to the night before. "The police say she was poisoned with antifreeze but I don't know how. I do know that she and her friend both seemed tipsy that last time I saw them. That wasn't long before she fell out of her chair dead."

"You say you saw the victim shortly before she died and she looked drunk?" Reese asked. "Did you notice anything else about her? Flushed skin? Heavy breathing? Dehydration?"

I tried to remember any impressions I'd had of Veronica when she'd joined us at the bar. "Not really. Aside from having a hard time walking straight, but then she'd been pregaming so we weren't surprised she was already half in the bag. We were all trying a cocktail one of the girls, Kristina, had come up with. The bartender made two of the cocktails for them, and then they took them back to their table with them."

"So someone could have slipped something in the drink?"

"I don't see how. I was right there when the bartender made them and passed them to Richard. And only one person died but the drinks were made together."

"How's Richard taking all this?" Reese asked.

"How do you think?" I said. "Hysterics, swooning, the works."

"So par for the course?" Reese laughed. He'd been around Richard enough to know that he did not do well in stressful situations. Even worse when stressful situations involved dead bodies. "So what about the second death?"

"We found her lying on a beach chair dead. All I know is she wasn't outside for very long because Fern and Kate saw her walk out and sit down after Richard and I left on a walk with the LA planners. We found her when we got back. We weren't gone for more than twenty minutes tops."

"So at this point there's no way to know if something happened to her before she came out or if she was killed when she was lying on the chair?"

"Not really." From the corner of my eye, I saw the Balinese police officer headed my way. "I think I need to go. It looks like the cops here want to talk to me."

"Annabelle," Reese's voice was insistent. "Be careful. I don't know how the police investigate crimes there, but I do know you do not want to get arrested in Indonesia."

"Why would I get arrested?" I cupped my hand over my mouth. "I'm just a witness."

"You have a talent for going from witness to suspect very quickly. Promise me you will not meddle in this case. I doubt the detectives there will be as understanding as me."

I wouldn't always classify him as understanding, but I kept my mouth shut and promised him that I would steer clear of the investigation. I hung up and turned around, finding myself face-to-face with a Balinese man about my height, his police hat tilted on his head and the gold of the badge shining in the sun.

He wasn't smiling. "I have some questions for the woman who found the body."

CHAPTER 12

"Thank heavens they let you go," Richard said as we walked across the pool deck into the hotel lobby.

"Why wouldn't they?" I tried to hide the relief I felt that my police interview had been perfunctory. "I barely knew the victim, and I wasn't anywhere near her when she died."

"Being held for questioning might not be so bad," Fern said. "A couple of those officers were cute. And those hats were fabulous."

"Too Gestapo for my taste," Richard said, looking back to where the officers still clustered around the body.

Fern wiggled his eyebrows up and down. "Exactly."

"Can we forget about your fondness for jack boots for a moment and focus on Annabelle?" Richard asked.

"I'm fine. Really. It was routine questioning." I didn't mention how worried I'd been that Jeremy might have tipped off the police about my involvement in other murder investigations and my brief stint as a person of interest in a case. Luckily, his threats seemed to have been a bunch of hot air. So far.

The lobby was nearly empty of guests, and I only spotted one waiter clearing a tea service from a low table. The soft background music gave an unnatural calm to the expansive room and served as a stark contrast to the activity and chatter of the beach. We crossed the marble floor, our flip-flops slapping against the surface. I slowed my pace and walked on my toes in an attempt to silence my shoes.

Before we reached the elevator bank that led up to our suites, I heard Buster and Mack trudging across the lobby. With their leather pants and vests covered in chains, it was nearly impossible for them to go anywhere in stealth mode. The sound of their leather and jangling of their metal preceded them. I nudged Kate as I turned to see the two men walking toward us, shoulders sagging. "This doesn't look good."

We met the pair as they reached the round marble entrance table topped with a lush arrangement of white lilies and whitewashed curly willow branches jutting out of the top. Mack smiled when he saw us, but it was a weak counterfeit of his usual wide grin.

"Who died?" Fern asked, then put his fingers to his lips and gave a nervous giggle. "Oops."

"I know it's awful to be so petty considering what happened," Mack said, "but the dinner at Sky Bar has been canceled, and we just finished the decor."

"That's the second event that's been a bust." Buster's voice was an even deeper rumble than usual. "This is getting discouraging."

"I thought you weren't doing much decor for tonight," Kate said.

Mack absentmindedly fiddled with the silver hoop piercing his eyebrow. "The tables weren't the focus since it was designed to be more of a cocktail party, but we came up with some fun design elements for the stations."

"Is it still set up?" Fern asked.

Buster nodded. "The hotel is having photos taken, so even if the party doesn't happen, they can use the images for marketing."

"Then why don't we go use it?" Fern asked. When we all stared at him, he continued. "It's a shame to let the work go to waste, and we have to eat. Why not order some food and eat it there?"

Richard shrugged. "It beats eating in our rooms."

Mack's face brightened. "Would you really do that?"

"Why not?" I said. "We don't even need to get dressed up."

He spun on his heel and beckoned for us to follow him. "It's just through here."

We walked from the lobby down a long hallway to a door that led outside. A sidewalk lined with low palms and flowering bushes took us to another section of the resort and around another pool. We passed a glass-walled restaurant and then went up a flight of marble steps.

"Voila!" Buster spread his arms wide when we reached the top of the stairs and the rooftop bar. From the second floor vantage point, we could see over the pool to the Indian Ocean where the fading sunlight cast a hue of gold over the teal-blue water. Sleek white rattan chairs and scoop-backed couches were arranged throughout the space around low square tables. White standing umbrellas dotted the perimeter of the rooftop while high-top metal tables ran along the glass-and-chrome railing.

A wall of greenery had been erected near the entrance, centered with a floating sign of the word "Cheers" in shiny gold script. An old-fashioned claw-foot bathtub filled with glass balls that looked like shimmering, oversized bubbles sat to one side.

"What's in the bubbles?" I asked when I noticed the glass balls weren't empty.

"Salad bites," Buster said, rocking back on his heels. "The bottom of the tub is filled with ice packs to keep them cold."

Kate picked up one of the bubbles, inspecting the leafy greens inside. "Pretty clever."

Richard plucked a miniature silver fork from the metal bath caddy stretched across the tub that held cocktail napkins and silverware, then picked up a salad bubble and took a taste. "Is this a tropical vinaigrette?"

Mack held up his hands. "We just do the decor. You'll have to ask the chef about the contents."

"I wonder if the chef would share his recipe?" Richard said. "I can't tell if this is papaya or something else. But whatever it is, it's out of this world."

I walked from the bathtub to a Plexiglas cube that held a display of fruits carved to look like flowers. "Who carved the mango to look like fish?"

Kate leaned close to the elaborate carvings. "And are the fish swimming through leaves cut from mango, too? It's like looking at a fruit diorama."

"All the chef's doing," Buster admitted. "And his staff. But what do you think of our floral life rings?"

He pointed above the bar to a pair of life rings made from pink roses in shades ranging from blush to soft pink to fuchsia. Below them sat a long, deep bucket made out of ice, filled with more ice and packed full of bottles.

I patted Buster on the back. "You and Mack did a great job. I'm sorry no one else will get to see this."

Richard pulled two bottles from the ice bucket and handed one to me. "I'm not normally a beer drinker, but I think today calls for it."

"Agreed." Kate grabbed two bottles by the neck and pulled them out, passing them to Fern before pulling out two more.

Buster and Mack twisted off their caps and raised the bottles in the air. "To this week getting better."

Fern clinked his bottle against mine. "Yes, please. I'm getting tired of dead bodies."

"Do you know who died today?" Mack asked as we made our way over to a cluster of low white furniture grouped around a wide table, a box of wheat grass adorning the center.

I took a seat on the long couch between Mack and Richard while Kate, Fern, and Buster each took chairs facing us.

"Do we know?" Kate jerked a finger in my direction. "Annabelle is the one who discovered the body."

Buster's jaw dropped. "What? We had no idea."

Mack put a hand on my knee. "Are you okay?"

I smiled at him, trying to force the image of the dead woman's face out of my mind. "I'm fine. It wasn't as bad as it sounds. Dina was on a lounge chair, and I tried to wake her up."

Buster scratched his bald head and the black motorcycle goggles he wore on top rode up a few inches. "Dina. Which one was she?"

"Pale with dark hair," Fern said. "She wore it up in a high bun last night. Probably to give her a poor woman's face lift."

Mack gave his head a shake. "I don't think we met her."

"She was friends with the other victim, Veronica," I said.

"The blonde with split ends," Fern said.

Richard arched a brow. "Someone has good eyes."

Fern fluttered his eyelashes. "It's a gift." He leaned over and patted Richard's shoulder. "And you could use a deep conditioning, sweetie."

Richard narrowed his eyes at Fern but put a hand to his dark, choppy hair. "We'd just walked up when Annabelle discovered Dina." He gestured to Kate and Fern. "These two were sitting a few chairs away from her the entire time."

Fern gasped, reaching for Kate with one hand. "He's right. We were only feet away from a corpse for who knows how long."

I'd been so caught up with the shock of realizing Dina was dead, then the chaos that followed calling hotel security, I'd forgotten two of my best friends were the closest witnesses. I thought back to the row of lounge chairs and the three empty ones separating Dina from Kate and Fern. "Was anyone sitting between you at any point?"

Kate reclined in her chair and swiveled it in a half circle so that she faced Fern. "I don't think so, do you?"

Fern tapped a finger to his temple. "Wasn't there someone between us when she arrived? But then they left right afterward?"

"Someone you recognized?" I asked.

Fern looked heavenward, shaking his head. "It might have been that talkative bride, but it's a bit fuzzy."

"Fuzzy because of all the drinks you had?" I tapped a foot on the marble floor. "Don't think I didn't notice the empty cocktail glasses when we came back."

Fern pressed a hand to his heart. "Are you implying that all those were mine?" He winked at me and laughed. "Honey, I wish. Those drinks were delicious, but half of those glasses were Kate's."

I turned my gaze on Kate.

"What?" she said. "It's not a crime to have a cocktail or two on the beach. It wasn't like I knew I'd need to remember everything because someone was going to turn up dead."

I let my shoulders relax a bit. "No, you're right. Hindsight is twenty-twenty."

"I can tell you that Dina talked to a few people on her way to her chair but not much more than saying hi," Kate said. "Once she picked out her chair and ordered her drinks, she wasn't very talkative. She seemed to want to be left alone."

Since her friend was murdered, I wasn't surprised she'd wanted a bit of solitude to go with her sun.

"We did recommend she try the elderflower and the lychee drinks," Fern added.

Kate nodded. "Because she asked about the frozen green drink Fern was drinking."

Fern closed his eyes as if remembering the cocktail. "The frozen lychee martini."

"And she ordered one?" I asked.

"The frozen one, yes," Fern said.

I thought back to the empty glasses on the table next to Dina. "But there were more than one empty glass when we found her."

"She said she was dying of thirst." Fern shivered. "We thought she was exaggerating, but I suppose not."

I thought back to Reese asking me if the victim had seemed dehydrated.

Kate snapped her fingers and looked at Fern. "She was sent a drink, remember?"

"That's right." He bobbed his head up and down at Kate. "And I told you that it was unfair that someone with those laugh lines was being sent a drink and we weren't."

I overlooked Fern's critique of the dead woman. "She was sent a drink? Are you sure?" Was this how she was killed? It would fit the killer's MO since Veronica had also been poisoned.

"Don't you remember?" Kate said to Fern. "Once we heard what the waiter said, we thought it was especially unfair."

Richard sat up. "What did the waiter say?"

"That the drink was a kickoff cocktail for tonight's dinner," Fern said, looking over his shoulder even though we were the only people on the rooftop bar. "Compliments of Carol Ann."

CHAPTER 13

"Clearly that was a lie," Richard said as we gathered in the lobby the next morning, continuing our conversation from the night before. "But why name Carol Ann?"

"Because Dina must have trusted Carol Ann enough to drink it," I said, tucking my pink T-shirt into my long black-jersey skirt and hiking my black Longchamp tote bag higher onto my shoulder.

"If Carol Ann had sent us a drink to kick off the evening, wouldn't we have drunk it?" Kate asked, slipping the spaghetti strap of her minidress back onto her shoulder.

She made a good point. Since Carol Ann was the trip organizer, it would have made sense. Not to mention that Dina probably knew Carol Ann from other wedding planner trips and conferences and would have trusted her.

"We need to question the bartender who delivered the drink," I turned to Kate and Fern. "Would you recognize him again if you saw him?"

Kate dug through her bag and produced a pair of oversized sunglasses. "Probably. Maybe."

Fern leaned against the round marble table and sighed. "The real question is, where is the coffee?"

"Very helpful, you two," I said.

"Isn't the real question what's going on with this outfit?" Richard waved a hand in front of Fern who arched an eyebrow at him as he adjusted his white Balinese hat so the fabric knot faced the front.

Even though Fern wore white Bermuda shorts and a white sweater tied around his shoulders, he'd managed to get his hands on a traditional black-and-white checked shirt and a red sash to go with his hat. "What? We're visiting a traditional Balinese town today, so I'm wearing a traditional Balinese outfit."

Richard gave him the once-over. "You look like a Balinese man who tripped and fell into a Ralph Lauren ad."

"At least I'm making an effort to meld with the culture," Fern said, crossing his arms.

Kate held up a hand. "Until I have some coffee, I'm not going to be able to meld with anything."

I pointed to the coffee station behind us and breathed in the rich aroma. I'd always loved the smell of coffee more than the taste, but the coffee in Bali was changing my mind. I recognized the baristas behind the cappuccino machines as the same men who'd made our coffee yesterday morning, and I followed Kate as she walked over.

"I'm with you," I said. "You-know-who called me again this morning."

"Nutso Natalie?" Kate asked. "Please tell me it wasn't at four a.m."

"It wasn't," I said. "It was at five."

Kate shook her head. "You're going to have to block her number."

"At least her wedding is only a month away," I said.

"And at least she gave up the idea of carrying her cat down the aisle in a basket." Kate scanned the chalkboard coffee sign. "I don't know if we have enough Bactine in our emergency kit for that."

I'd gotten used to having dogs at weddings, but drew the line at cats, ferrets, and any other pet that didn't readily follow commands. Not that all of our dog ring bearers had been angels, I thought, remembering chasing a pair of Jack Russell terriers (and the platinum wedding rings they wore around their necks) through two parks before catching them.

"Why are we the first ones down here?" Kate asked after we'd both placed our orders.

"I might have told you an earlier start time," I said, not meeting her eyes, "to make sure you were ready on time."

She took the to-go coffee cup from the barista and glared at me over the top as she took a sip. "Have I mentioned how evil you are?"

"A few times." I cupped my hands around the cardboard sleeve on my vanilla latte and let the warmth seep into my fingers. Even though Bali had no shortage of heat, the warmth of the coffee felt soothing.

Richard eyed my coffee when we rejoined them. "Don't forget that we have a long car ride ahead of us."

"How long does it take to reach Ubud?" Kate asked.

Richard pulled his guidebook out of the black crossbody bag he wore slung across his chest. Usually his little Yorkie, Hermes, rode in the bag, and I missed seeing the black-and-brown furry head poking out. I had not missed the experience of a long-haul flight with an energetic dog, so I was grateful Richard had left Hermes with my nutty neighbor, Leatrice. "I can't tell from the map, but at least an hour."

Kate took a swallow of coffee. "Are Buster and Mack joining us?"

"Don't you remember?" I asked. "They told us last night that they would be going ahead of us to set up the decor for the lunch."

"That must have been after a few of those Indonesian beers,"

Kate said, rubbing her forehead. "Do you think I'll be able to nap on the drive up?"

"I wonder if we'll have the same type of vans we took to the waterfall and temple," Fern said. "Those vans were set up for napping."

"Wonder no longer," I said as I heard the low rumble of multiple cars approaching the portico off the open lobby.

Fern clapped his hands as a row of cars appeared. "This is much better than vans."

Vividly colored vintage Jeep buggies with convertible tops pulled up and idled in front of us, each one decorated with a cluster of matching balloons tied to the front bumper.

Kate's mouth fell open. "I guess we're not going incognito, and I guess I'm not getting my nap."

"Are those cars for us?" Alan asked as he joined our group, linking his muscular arm through mine. "Ripper!"

Richard gave him a dismissive glance. "Where were you yesterday?"

"I heard about all the commotion on the beach." Alan grimaced. "I stayed in my room to get some work done on my lappy. I have a big event coming up in Sydney." He patted my hand. "Was it awful?"

I shrugged, trying not to dwell on the moment I pulled Dina's sunglasses off her face and stared into her lifeless eyes. "It was disturbing."

Alan shook his head. "Hard to believe another person carked it."

Between Alan's Aussie speak and Kate's routine mangling of expressions, I was fast on my way to needing a personal translator.

"You know a couple of Australians died here in Bali when bartenders watered down drinks with antifreeze?" Alan rubbed his arms as if trying to warm up. "Horrid way to go."

"What happened to watering drinks down with water the good, old-fashioned way?" Kate asked.

Richard sniffed. "I don't think this is a case of bad bartending."

"Let's hope not." Fern put a hand to his throat. "I'd hate to have to cut back on cocktails."

"Don't worry," Richard said. "If the bartenders here were serving antifreeze in every drink, you'd be dead already."

Fern gave a sigh of relief, then the smile slipped off his face, and he made a face at Richard. "Hilarious."

Alan looked at us. "You all seem to be handling it well."

Kate winked at Alan. "It's not our first rodeo."

"Should we pick our cars?" I asked before Alan could question what Kate meant. Other planners were starting to gather behind us, and I did not want to get stuck in long conversations about Dina and how we'd found her body.

Carol Ann strode through the group with Dahlia running behind her, the Plexiglas clipboard clutched tightly in hand.

"Good morning, everyone." Carol Ann's voice was artificially cheery and her smile almost disturbingly bright. "These fun buggies will take you up to Ubud for the day. Each vehicle holds three people, but I'd like you to split yourselves up so you're not riding with people you traveled here with." When there was a quiet groan throughout the group, Carol Ann raised her voice. "The point of this trip is to make friends and meet new people. It's no fun if you stay with the same people all the time. Mingle, people. Mingle."

Richard huffed. "I have all the friends I need, thank you very much."

I patted him on the arm. "This won't kill you. And you might meet someone fun."

"If I get stuck with Jeremy, I'm throwing myself out of the car," Richard said as he stalked off toward the Jeeps.

"I second that," Kate spotted Kristina who'd just walked up. "See you on the other side."

I watched the trip's cutest couple, Jacob and Katherine, reluctantly part ways and head to separate buggies, and, for a moment, I wished Reese was with me. I shook the thought from my head and grabbed Alan's hand as I made a beeline for a Creamsicle-orange buggy. "Come on. We didn't travel here together. It counts as mingling."

I opened the door to the backseat and slid in while Alan hopped in the front, next to the driver. I saw Brett walking down the lobby steps to the row of cars, but before I could call out to him to join us, the door to the other side of the buggy opened and Sasha sat down next to me, accompanied by a cloud of Shalimar perfume.

She appraised me and then Alan. "I suppose this is as good as any, although why we aren't riding in air-conditioned coaches is beyond me."

I tried to hide my disappointment at the prospect of an hour trapped in a small car with the brassy planner. "Don't you think these vintage Jeeps are fun?"

She flipped her bright-red hair behind her and a few strands caught me in the face. "I expected limousines, not buggies."

"Have a go. It's an adventure." Alan gave her his sweetest smile before turning to face forward.

Our Balinese driver got in the car and the processional of Jeeps began to move in front of us. We pulled out of the portico behind a neon-green buggy and snaked our way up the curved drive, passing through the massive entrance walls covered in dark-brown rosettes. We turned out of the resort and drove through the area of Nusa Dua until we merged onto a highway that looked brand new and was virtually free from traffic.

The hum of the vintage motor made it hard for me to talk to Alan, so I turned to Sasha. "Are you enjoying the trip so far?" That seemed like an innocuous question.

She gave a derisive laugh. "I'd hardly call this a successful FAM trip. Haven't you noticed all the wedding planners dropping dead?"

I fought the urge to give her a snarky response. "Yes, but I thought you wouldn't mind at least one of them being dead."

She narrowed her eyes at me. "What does that mean?"

I decided to go for broke since we were zipping along the highway, and there was no way she could escape my questioning. "Oh, nothing. I did hear that you and Veronica once fought over the same man."

Alan swiveled his neck around, his blue eyes wide.

"The gossip mill's still working well, I see." Sasha dug in her oversized Louis Vuitton purse and produced her cigarette holder and electric cigarette. "It's no secret she took my sloppy seconds, but it's not something I'd kill over."

"I heard that you were upset enough to stop attending Inspire."

Sasha took a drag from the end of the long white holder. "I'll admit that I may have wanted to get even with her when it happened, but that was years ago. I'm not the kind of woman who waits five years to take my revenge."

Alan mouthed the word 'wow' to me when Sasha turned her head to the window to blow out imaginary smoke. I nodded at him and mouthed 'I know.'

I turned my attention to the scenery as we exited the highway and began driving through villages. Houses sat close to the two-lane road and were interspersed with open-air shops, some with roll-down metal doors. I spotted a few homes with their own temples tucked behind wrought iron gates. The front of the homes and businesses were strewn with the remains of morning offerings: the vivid flower blossoms, bits of food, and bamboo baskets placed outside every doorway to appease the Hindu gods. I leaned my head out of the car window and could smell the lingering scent of incense that had burned in the offerings.

"It's not like I've missed much at Inspire," Sasha continued. "It's the same people, the same cliques."

"But you haven't been in five years," I said, turning my face to her and breathing in fruity vapor from the fake cigarette combined with the heavy perfume I assumed she bathed in. At least it was better than a lung full of smoke.

"Jeremy updated me on everything, and, according to him, I didn't miss anything." She tapped her holder on the open car window and I half expected ash to fall to the ground.

"Since Jeremy went, he must have known both of the victims pretty well," I said. "Was he in their clique?"

"Not anymore." Sasha leaned back against the seat. "He had a falling out with Veronica and Dina a couple of years ago. Cathy, too."

It wasn't hard for me to imagine other planners disliking Jeremy since I despised him so much. What was hard to believe was the fact that he'd been friends with any of them. Usually you had to be a likable person to make friends, and Jeremy was in no way likable.

"Do you know why they fell out?" I asked.

Sasha studied me for a second. "They dropped him. He never told me why, but I do know that they cut him out of their group text chain and got him blacklisted from FAM trips they were invited to."

"Did it have to do with the scandal Veronica and Dina were involved with at Inspire a few years back?"

"If it did, he never told me. Then again, Jeremy isn't one to trash people behind their backs."

It took all my restraint not to laugh out loud. Trashing people behind their backs seemed to be one of Jeremy's specialties. If he had been involved and had incriminating evidence on the two women, I wondered why he hadn't told Sasha or used it against Veronica and Dina. Of course I knew the answer to that question.

He'd been biding his time so he could kill them instead. Knowing Jeremy the way I did, I did not put murder past him.

CHAPTER 14

"**D**id you hear all that?" I asked Alan as we got out of our Jeep in front of the Ubud monkey forest. Sasha had walked away to find Jeremy, leaving behind a trail of Shalimar and sickly sweet vapor from her fake cigarette.

"Only bits and pieces," Alan admitted, raising his tan muscular arms over his head to stretch. "I was distracted when our driver chucked a U-ey in the middle of the road."

I nodded, assuming he meant the U-turn our procession of cars had made. "Well, she all but admitted to me that her buddy Jeremy knew both victims well and had a good reason to want them dead." I scanned the row of orange, green, and red vintage buggies behind ours as other guests disembarked and began walking toward the park entrance. "I need to tell my crew."

Alan came around to my side of the car. "I'm getting the sense that you and your mates have a history with this guy Jeremy."

"We had the misfortune of working with him on a wedding once," I admitted, waving my arms wildly as I spotted Kate and Fern standing next to the stone sign at the entrance to the overgrown jungle. I pulled Alan with me as I hurried to join them.

"I hope you had a better ride up than I did," Kate said once we'd reached her.

"Don't bet on it," I said. "We were with Sasha. Who were you with?"

Kate put a finger to her ear and shook it. "Let me just say that Chatty Cathy comes by her nickname honestly."

"Well, I had a lovely ride up with Cliff and Ted," Fern said, straightening his Balinese hat. "They really are Renaissance men, you know."

"The owners of *Insider Weddings?*" I said, jealous that I'd missed a chance to get to know the two men better. I scanned the people walking past us into the forest. "Where's Richard?"

"I think I saw him walk ahead with Carol Ann and her assistants," Kate said.

Alan glanced down at his bare arm as if he wore a watch. "Should we get going? We only have thirty minutes inside before we're supposed to be back at the cars."

I zipped my black bag closed and tucked my long ponytail into the back of my pink T-shirt as we walked past the ornately carved stone sign announcing the entrance to the Sacred Monkey Forest Sanctuary and warning guests not to play with the wild monkeys. We followed the paved walkway shaded by a high canopy of leafy trees as gray long-tailed monkeys scampered across the path and perched on the stone ledge lining the walk. The air was cool and smelled loamy the further we walked into the overgrown jungle. Spongy moss covered rock walls, making the man-made structures seem to glow green as the slanting sun reached them through the treetops.

"It's beautiful," I whispered, feeling the sacredness of the space.

Alan pulled me closer to him and pointed to a large monkey following us. "If you don't mind being stalked."

"I'm going to buy some bananas." Kate motioned to a nearby stall with a peaked roof.

Fern strode ahead to an opening with a stone fountain where

monkeys sat grooming themselves and eyeing people as they passed. "We should be getting close to one of the temples."

I sidestepped a pair of monkeys running past me and approached a wooden post with directional arrows and a baby monkey perched on top. Luckily, the signs were in both Indonesian and English. "The holy spring temple is this way."

Kate ran up to us, holding a small bunch of slightly bruised bananas in each hand. "Want to feed them with me?"

Alan's eyes widened. "They just spotted your bananas, mate."

Before Kate could pass us a banana, two monkeys climbed up her legs and snatched the bunches from her hands. One of the monkeys continued on to her shoulders where he sat and peeled his bananas while the other monkey leapt down to the ground and ran away, dragging the yellow bunch of fruit with him.

Kate's mouth was a perfect O as she hunched her neck forward. "He's heavier than I would have guessed."

Alan and I both took a few steps back as the monkey settled himself on Kate and calmly devoured his snack.

"Does he look like he wants to get down?" Kate asked, her eyes swiveling to the side as she tried to look at her passenger.

"Maybe." I didn't want to tell Kate that her monkey friend looked like he was perfectly happy to spend the rest of the day sitting on her shoulders. Before I had to figure out how to create a distraction worthy of a monkey, the creature bounded down to the ground and ran off in pursuit of another person holding a banana.

Kate smoothed her dress, wiping off the marks from the dirty feet that had climbed over her. "Check that off my list of things never to do again."

I led the way down a series of winding wooden steps that twisted through the forest then rose again in front of a stone bridge flanked by a pair of moss-covered dragon statues. I let my hand rest on the wet moss as I walked up the slippery steps and across the bridge, avoiding the dangling tendrils of jungle roots hanging from the tall trees above us. I looked up and saw a curtain of roots blocking the sun as it attempted to peek through the thick foliage.

Fern leaned over a stone barrier to peer into a square pool below filled with dark, still water and floating leaves. "Well, that's not pretty."

"Where did Richard run off to?" I asked once we'd walked around the holy spring temple and were headed back up the wooden staircase.

"Forget Richard," Kate said. "Where's the rest of the group? I do not want to be left to live out the rest of my days with these banana-stealing monkeys."

Alan laughed and nudged Kate. "You spoil me."

"Is that Australian?" I asked, hoping to get a handle on Aussie slang by the end of the trip..

He shook his head. "Just Alan speak."

Kate grinned at him. "I like it. I may have to steal it."

I paused when we reached the open paved area with the stone fountain. "Does that sound like Richard?"

We turned and watched openmouthed as Richard ran past us waving his arms as he swatted a baby monkey sitting on his head and clinging to his hair. A larger monkey, whom I assumed was the baby's mother, chased after Richard, howling with her teeth bared.

"You must be out of your mind!" Richard screamed as he ran, splashing through the fountain and down the path toward the exit.

"I think we found him," Alan said.

"Now that's something you don't see everyday." Fern turned to us. "Did anyone get that on video?"

"Come on." I broke into a jog. "We'd better help him before he runs all the way back to the resort with that baby monkey on his head."

"That," Kate said, trying to catch up to me, "would be amazing."

We reached the entrance to the forest and found Richard bent over with his hands on his knees next to a small Balinese man dressed in a traditional black-and-white checked shirt. Thankfully, there was no sign of the baby monkey or its mother.

Richard looked up as we approached, his face flushed red. "Where were you all while I was being terrorized by a rabid ape?"

"You ran past us," Kate said, "but you were going too fast for us to do anything."

Richard jerked a thumb in the direction of the man next to him as he gasped for breath. "If this gentleman hadn't waved his slingshot, I would have been monkey food."

The man smiled at us and nodded, holding up his wooden slingshot. "Scares them off."

Fern sidled up next to the man in his identical black-and-white-checked shirt and red sash. The only difference was Fern's white sweater tied jauntily over his shoulders and his pristine Bermuda shorts. The man did a bit of a double take, then smiled widely at Fern's outfit.

"You know what?" Fern untied his sweater. "I think this would look fabulous on you. May I?"

The man nodded and continued smiling as Fern knotted the white sweater around his shoulders.

Fern took a step back to admire his handiwork. "Just as I thought. The sweater really does make the outfit."

"Can we please go?" Richard asked, straightening up. "I think I've had my fill of nature for the year." He thanked the slingshot man again as we left. The man waved and bowed at Fern.

"So where did you go inside the monkey forest?" I asked Richard as we walked toward the row of vintage buggies, the bundles of balloons tied to their front bumpers moving in the breeze. Kate, Fern, and Alan had walked ahead of us, and I knew Richard was walking deliberately slow to put more distance between them and us. "We looked for you everywhere."

"I was with Carol Ann, Kelly, and Dahlia. They're all quite

lovely, you know, and poor Carol Ann is just sick over these murders." Richard put a hand on my arm. "Dahlia is trying to hold everything together for Carol Ann, but I'm not sure if she's up to it. She's a little blonde, if you know what I mean."

"Do you mean ditzy?"

"Maybe," Richard scratched his chin "Sometimes I think she's a little spacey, but other times she seems very focused. I do know that the stress of the murders and having to manage her boss is giving her an eye twitch."

"That's not a good sign." I could only imagine how much pressure the girl must be under since this was her first job out of college.

"I'll tell you one thing. It may be the retro glasses influencing me, but that Kelly seems very mature for an intern."

"The glasses do make me think she's older," I agreed. "Is there anything we can do to help them?"

"I know one thing we shouldn't do." Richard leaned against the top of the nearest red Jeep. "Muddle up the investigation."

"That reminds me, has Carol Ann heard anything from the police about Dina's cause of death?"

Richard sighed. "Did you not hear the words that just left my mouth, Annabelle?"

I waved away his concerns. "I have no intention of meddling. I was merely curious. Can't a person be curious?"

Richard rapped his fingers along the black convertible top of the car. "Fine. Apparently, the cause of the death was the same for Dina as for Veronica."

"So just like we thought," I said, dropping my voice as other planners began emerging from the monkey forest and heading for the buggies. "They were both poisoned. Does Carol Ann know that the drink that probably poisoned Dina was supposedly a gift from her?"

Richard opened the car door on his side. "Since I didn't want her to have a nervous breakdown in the monkey forest, I thought it best not to bring that up. But traces of antifreeze were found around her water bottle as well as the martini glass."

"The water bottle?" I thought back to the pink Sigg bottle I'd noticed in her beach bag. "So she'd been drinking poison the whole time she worked out without knowing it? How is that possible?"

"Carol Ann told me it was common knowledge Dina put flavor drops in her water. Never went anywhere without them. Couldn't stand the taste of plain water."

"Common knowledge to anyone who knew her from Inspire," I said. "We didn't know."

"I guess you can cross us off your suspect list then," Richard said.

"Ha ha." I tapped my chin while I thought. "If the poison was in the water, then the poisoned drink was either backup or used to frame Carol Ann or both. If Carol Ann had wanted to kill Dina, she wouldn't have implicated herself like that."

"Unless that was part of the ruse," Richard said.

I stared at Richard. "Do you really think Carol Ann could have pulled that off?"

"Of course not. I was just playing devil's advocate."

I stepped up onto the running board and leaned over the top of the car. "Did you know that Jeremy Johns was part of the same Inspire clique as Veronica and Dina, but they dropped him after they were all involved in some sort of scandal?"

"What kind of a scandal?"

I looked around me to see if anyone was within earshot. I spotted Alan waving at me from further down the row as he got into a green Jeep with Kate and Fern, so I waved back then turned my attention back to Richard. "Some kind of sex scandal, I think."

Richard wrinkled his nose. "With Jeremy?"

"I know it's not pretty to think about," I said. "But from what Sasha said, they dropped him from the group and he was furious. And we've all seen what Jeremy's like when he loses his temper."

"You think he killed them?" Richard asked, then stamped one foot on the ground. "Wait, why am I even debating this with you? I'm supposed to be keeping you from poking around in the case. I promised to keep you out of this."

I held up a hand. "You promised? Who did you promise?" I narrowed my eyes at him as his cheeks flushed red and his eyes darted away from mine. "Have you been talking to Reese behind my back?"

CHAPTER 15

"I take the fifth," Richard said, opening the car door and popping out the second it came to a stop alongside the road.

I followed him out of the Jeep. "And that's the fifth time you've said that since I asked you if you've been talking to Detective Reese behind my back."

We'd only been riding in the vintage buggies for a few minutes since leaving the monkey forest, but our driver had announced that we'd arrived at the rice paddy overlook where we were having lunch. I concluded that we must still be near the town of Ubud since we'd only driven a few miles, and I knew Ubud was renowned for its terraced rice paddies.

I waited for a stream of cars to pass before I could cross the road to follow Richard, coughing a bit from the exhaust fumes. Ubud had more traffic than I expected, by foot and by car, and I dodged a group of women carrying yoga mats once I'd reached the other side of the road. One thing that Bali did not seem to have was people honking their car horns. No matter the traffic jam, Balinese drivers didn't touch their horns. I considered this a mark in the win column for the island.

I walked a few steps down, following the wooden signs for the restaurant and the disappearing form of Richard. As I turned and stepped out onto a wooden platform covered by a thatched roof, I forgot about chasing down my friend and took a moment to take in the breathtaking vista.

The restaurant overlooked a wide hill sloping toward us in a series of terraces cut into the soil, making it look like a verdant staircase. The top of the hill was covered in thick vegetation with tall palm trees springing up from the base. The terraces undulated around the curves of the hill, the stalks of the growing rice creating a carpet of bright green as far as I could see. Where the terraced steps weren't green, they were soaked with water, tiny shoots of rice plants barely breaking the surface. I breathed in the moist air, wondering if it would soon rain.

"You made it!" Buster's rumbling voice jerked me out of my moment's peace.

I jerked my head to the left and saw him standing with Mack next to a long rectangular table that stretched from one end of the covered platform to the other. The platform itself jutted out over the terraced rice fields, giving me the sensation of floating above them. The table had been draped in a white-linen cloth that reached the floor and was surrounded by rattan chairs. A low wooden trough of moss extended down the middle of the table and was dotted with white orchids. In front of each chair lay a place mat woven out of green palm fronds, and on top of that sat a square white basket covered with a lid and tied with a white tag. I bent over one of the tags and read a name in gold swirling calligraphy that shimmered in the sunlight.

"Did you do all of this?" I asked, straightening up and giving them both a quick peck on the cheek. Both men wore their usual black leather pants, but white Balinese shirts with short sleeves, Nehru collars, and brown buttons had replaced their vests with chains. It was a jolting combination.

Mack held up his hands. "I might have gotten carpal tunnel syndrome from all the weaving."

"We kept the decor low since the view is the main attraction," Buster said.

I glanced again at the sweeping rice terraces. "I can see what you mean. You don't want anything to block this vista."

Mack leaned close to whisper in my ear. "The seats are assigned, but we were able to switch you around so you aren't sitting anywhere near Jeremy or Sasha again."

"Thanks," I said, although I wouldn't have minded getting a chance to question Jeremy about just how vengeful he'd felt toward the two murder victims.

I looked down the row of chairs to where Richard had taken his spot next to Chatty Cathy, nodding as she talked to him. He must really want to avoid my questions about Reese if he was voluntarily subjecting himself to her verbal onslaught. I decided to drop my questioning for the moment and enjoy the lunch and the surroundings. The last thing I wanted to do was to miss experiencing Bali because I was obsessed with the murder investigation and Jeremy Johns.

"You're over here, Annabelle," Kate called from the far end of the table, motioning to a seat between her and Brett that faced the overlook.

When I reached the chair, Brett patted it. "I haven't gotten a chance to talk to you since yesterday. Are you okay?"

I nodded as I sat down next to him. "I'd rather not find any more dead bodies, but I'm fine."

"You and me both." Brett winked at me, the skin around his eyes crinkling, and I noticed for the first time how blue his eyes were. Combined with his blond hair and tan, they made him quintessentially Californian.

"Did you know that Dina only drank flavored water?" I asked, trying to keep my voice light.

"Sure," he said, untying the ribbon around his box. "She even carried those little squeeze bottles of flavor drops in her purse. Like one of those people who carries around their own salad dressing."

"So it was common knowledge?"

Brett laughed. "I think anyone who ever shared a meal with her would have noticed."

So much for narrowing down the field.

Kate took the seat next to me, and Fern waved from across the table where he sat next to a woman I didn't recognize with feathery brown hair. I tried to catch Richard's eye, but he seemed unable to escape his conversation with Cathy. Jacob and Katherine were together again, and I spotted Alan sitting next to Kristina. He pointed to the silver flask peaking out of his shirt pocket as he raised his eyebrows at me. I smiled and shook my head, although the idea of a spiked drink was appealing. Although it might be nice to take the edge off interacting with some people, I wanted to keep my head clear as I pondered potential suspects.

A hand reached around me, unfurling my napkin and draping it across my lap. I twisted around and couldn't help being surprised when I recognized one of the waiters from our resort. I turned all the way around and realized that all of the waiters were from our resort.

"They bussed them in," Brett said when he noticed my expression.

"Our waiters followed us to Ubud?" Kate asked, following my gaze at the row of waiters standing behind us in white Nehru jackets and black pants.

Like Buster's and Mack's outfits minus the leather, I thought.

"Have you looked inside your box?" Brett asked me.

I wiggled the cover off the square basket and set it to the side. Inside was an artfully arranged box lunch with sealed containers of salad, cold noodles, and French macarons in a range of pastels. "Was the food transported here with the waiters?"

"I think so." Brett popped open the plastic lid to his noodles.

Kate nudged me in the side. "That's him."

"That's who?"

Kate pointed to a waiter standing against the wall. "That's the waiter who delivered the drink to Dina yesterday."

I studied the Balinese man with shiny black hair parted neatly to one side. "Are you sure?"

Kate narrowed her eyes. "Pretty sure. He was also one of the bartenders at the welcome dinner."

"So he's been at the scenes of both murders?"

"Yes," Kate said. "But so have a lot of people in this room, including us."

I pushed my chair back from the table. "Touché."

"You're going to talk to him now?" Kate asked, glancing around as people began eating.

"No time like the present."

I walked around the table to where the man stood, his hands clasped in front of him.

"Can I help you with something?" he asked.

"I hope so," I said, trying to keep my voice low so it couldn't be overheard. "You were serving drinks yesterday at the beach, right."

He nodded, but looked wary.

"You were told to deliver a drink to the woman who died, right?"

His face paled. "I already talked to the police."

"I know. I just wanted to know who asked you to deliver it. Do you remember what they looked like?"

He shook his head. "The request was written out on hotel letterhead and was sitting on a tray with the drink when I came back to the service station. It looked official to me."

"And you didn't see anyone put it there?"

Another shake of the head. It was clear from the man's face that he knew nothing. I thanked him and returned to my seat.

Kate looked at my expression. "No luck?"

"The delivery request was written on hotel letterhead. He didn't see the person who left it or the drink."

Kate tapped her bamboo fork against the side of her basket. "That does tell us one thing. It wasn't a crime of passion. The killer is good at planning."

I looked up and down the long table. "So that narrows our suspect list down to everyone."

CHAPTER 16

"N ot everyone," Kate said. "For one thing, we know it wasn't any of our team. And I doubt Carol Ann would sabotage her own trip."

"And the guys from *Insider Weddings* wouldn't sponsor a trip just to go on a killing spree," I added. "Plus, they're way too sophisticated and charming to be murderers."

"So we're looking for an unsophisticated, ill-mannered rube among a group of world-renowned wedding planners?" Kate asked. "That should be easy."

Kate made a good point. No one on this trip fit the mold of serial killer. I removed my box of macarons, setting them to the side as I peered down the length of the table. Everyone from our group had taken a seat, and I spotted Jeremy at the other end of the table next to Dahlia. The blond assistant did not look thrilled to be beside him, and even from this distance I noticed her left eye twitch.

"Has Carol Ann's assistant ever been to Inspire?" I asked, turning in my seat to face Brett.

Brett scanned the table until he spotted Dahlia, then shook his head. "The blonde who looks perpetually overwhelmed? Nope. I don't think she's worked for Carol Ann for more than a year tops, and this is her first job. Why?"

"She doesn't look happy to be next to Jeremy. I wondered if she'd met him before or if her dislike was new to this trip."

Brett stirred his noodles with his bamboo fork. "That guy? I don't think anyone is happy to be stuck talking to him whether they've met him before or not. Luckily, I knew to steer clear after knowing him at Inspire."

"But you didn't hang out with his group?" I asked, waiting for Brett to swallow his bite before he could answer.

He shook his head. "Not by a long shot. Any group whose sole purpose is to hook up and convince other people to do the same is not for me."

I cringed. "Is that what their big sex scandal was about?"

"Which one? I feel like they caused a scandal just about every year. Usually by themselves, but sometimes they liked to play matchmaker."

I opened my square plastic container of salad then hunted around the bottom of my box for the fork. "Do you remember why the other people in the group decided to ostracize Jeremy?"

Brett shifted in his seat. "Did they? I guess I wasn't hooked in enough to know the details."

"It just seems coincidental that two of the women Jeremy used to pal around with turn up dead after they stop being friends with him."

"Don't get me wrong," Brett said, "I'm not a fan of Jeremy's, but do you think he would kill two people over a spat at a wedding conference?"

I thought Jeremy Johns would kill someone for stealing his parking space, but I didn't say that to Brett. I took a bite of mixed greens tossed in coconut vinaigrette and marveled at how crisp the leaves were. Had they packed these boxes in ice? As I took another bite of the refreshing salad, I looked down the table and noticed that Dahlia had left her seat.

"I'll be right back," I said to Kate.

"Where are you going now?"

"I want to talk to Jeremy. I think he has more of a motive than he's been letting on."

"Are you sure that's such a good idea?" Kate dropped her voice. "People have already heard that we've been involved in murder investigations before. It might not look so good for us to be poking around."

I waved away her concerns. "I'm not poking around in the case. I just want to talk to him."

"Isn't that six in one, six dozen the other?"

I paused for a moment. "Something like that."

I left Kate and made a beeline for the vacant chair next to Jeremy, pausing to sidestep a waiter. Jeremy spotted me and we locked eyes, then he pushed away from the table, knocking his chair to the floor. I picked up the chair as I passed by, following Jeremy as he hurried down a spiral staircase at the end of the platform. I cursed under my breath. Why was he running from me?

When I reached the bottom of the stairs, I was on ground level with the rice paddies extending below me then rising up the hillside. I swept my gaze across the field and spotted Jeremy dodging behind some low bushes with wide fan-like leaves. I followed him, pushing back the foliage to reveal a dirt path leading down and saw Jeremy skidding down it.

"I just want to talk to you," I called out to him.

He turned around, leveling a finger at me. "Leave me alone. I have nothing to say to you or your crazy crew."

"Hey," I said, putting my hands on my hips. "My crew isn't crazy. Especially since Leatrice isn't with us. And why are you mad at me? You're the one who's been talking trash about us."

"I know what you're up to. You're trying to pin all this on me because I knew those two floozies. Well, I've worked too hard to build my name back up to let that happen." He gave me a look of pure venom and took off across one of the terraced rows.

I sighed but decided to follow him. If he was this upset, he must have something to do with the murders. Or at least know something.

I took the slope at a run, holding my arms out for balance, and paused at the bottom to right myself.

"Look out below," Mack said moments before I turned to see him barreling down the steep path with Buster fast on his heels.

I jumped out of their way and they stumbled past me, catching each other before they careened off one of the grassy ledges. "What are you guys doing?"

"It looked like you might need some help," Buster said, pointing at Jeremy's retreating back.

Mack grinned. "And we're good at tackling people."

"I know." I remembered very well the duo capturing a suspect in a past investigation by landing on top of him. "But I don't want to make a scene. I just want to ask Jeremy a couple of questions."

"Just in case you need someone to tackle him, we're here," Mack assured me.

Since Buster and Mack despised Jeremy Johns as much as any of us, I knew they were hoping for an opportunity to face plant him in a rice paddy.

"Then let's go." Buster waved for me to follow him, so I ran after the two beefy men as they lumbered across the rice fields.

Jeremy looked back and shrieked when he saw the three of us approaching.

"Why is he running?" Buster asked over his shoulder.

I wasn't sure why he'd taken off running from me in the first place, but I could understand why he ran now. Being chased by two three-hundred-pound bikers, albeit ones who belonged to a Christian biker gang, might make me want to run.

I felt the ground tremble as Buster and Mack pounded down the dirt path. Jeremy looked over his shoulder again, letting out a high-pitched yelp before he stumbled and went down face first in a soggy plot of rice seedlings. I skidded to a stop, cringing as

Mack, who couldn't contain his grin, lifted the fussy designer from the mud.

"Look what you've done," Jeremy spluttered. "My suit is ruined."

I shook my head. "It isn't my fault you ran. All I wanted to do was ask you a couple of questions about the two victims."

Jeremy wiped at his dripping face with a wet hand. "You don't know when to mind your own business, do you? I didn't have anything to do with those murders, but you want to know something?" He jerked his arm out of Mack's grip. "Those two women got what they deserved. I'm not the only person here who knows why, either. And if you're not careful, you'll get what you deserve just like they did."

With that he stomped off, leaving me with my mouth open.

CHAPTER 17

"I t was like watching a slow speed car chase," Kate said, flopping across my bed once we'd returned to the resort.

I dropped my tote on the marble floor near the nightstand and crossed to the sliding glass door, pushing it open and sucking in the salt-tinged air as I listened to the sounds of people splashing in the pool below. I looked over the tops of the palm trees to the turquoise blue of the ocean, shimmering as the setting sun reflected gold off its surface, and I felt my body begin to relax from the stress of the day. Between the car ride with Sasha, the aggressive monkeys, and the scene with Jeremy, my experience in Ubud had not been the relaxing and centering experience I'd hoped it would be. I sat down in the low chair next to the bed, rubbing my fingers back and forth against the nubby beige upholstery fabric.

"So everyone on the trip watched it?" My cheeks flamed as I remembered turning around after Jeremy had stormed off and seeing all the guests of the FAM trip gathered at the railing of the platform. Most memorable had been Richard's stormy expression.

"Pretty much. We heard Jeremy scream, then we all ran to the side as you and Buster and Mack chased him into a mud puddle."

"That was a rice paddy," I said. "And it wasn't technically our fault that he lost his footing and fell."

"Maybe not." Kate let her shoes drop to the floor. "But it was hilarious. Didn't you hear some of us clapping?"

"I'm guessing Richard was not one of those people?" I'd seen the hard line of his lips before he'd turned away from me with a flounce. Much like Jeremy, Richard liked to make a dramatic exit.

"I'm sure he'll come around," Kate said. "You know Richard and his moods."

That I did. One person walkouts were his signature move, triggered by anything from me having fake butter in my refrigerator to Kate mentioning the word Kardashian. "Did you know that he'd been talking to Reese behind my back?"

Kate sat up and scooted herself up so she could lean against the pile of fluffy white pillows stacked along the headboard. "Who? Richard? No way. I didn't think he even liked Reese."

"He mentioned something about promising to keep me out of trouble and away from the investigation. Who else could he have promised that to?"

"That does sound like something Reese has told you to do a few hundred times." Kate pulled one of her spaghetti straps back on her shoulder. "But it also sounds like Richard. Are you sure he didn't pretend someone told him to keep you out of trouble?"

I shook my head. "For one, he accidentally told me and looked panicked when he realized he did. And, two, Richard never lies to me."

Despite the fact that he refused to tell me his actual age, Richard was truthful to a fault. He was one of the few people I could always count on to tell it to me straight.

"You're right. He doesn't." Kate tapped a finger against the crisp-white duvet. "Not that I'd mind a little white lie every so often. I mean is it so hard to say 'no' when I ask if an outfit makes me look cheap?"

I grinned thinking of Richard's tough-love honesty. "Do you think I should back off and stay out of the investigation?"

Kate crossed her bare legs Indian style in front of her, leaning her elbow against her knees. "I think it's a stretch to say that you're meddling in the investigation. What have you actually done? Talked to a few people? Asked a few questions to see how everyone is connected to the victims? That's natural curiosity, especially considering we discovered the second body. Meddling would be withholding evidence from the cops or running a stakeout operation in front of a suspect's house. Both of which you've done in the past."

I felt my face flush again. "That's not fair. Withholding the evidence was an accident since I didn't know I had it, and the stakeout was really more Leatrice's idea."

Kate shrugged. "You know what they say. The road to hell is paved with good inventions."

"I do *not* know they say that," I muttered to myself, knowing how pointless it was to correct her.

"I miss having Leatrice around," Kate said. "She always keeps things lively."

That was an understatement.

"I, for one, am glad she's back home taking care of Richard's dog," I said.

"What are the over-under odds that she has him doing circus tricks like a seal by the time we get back?" Kate asked.

"About the same that the two of them will have an entire matching wardrobe."

Kate rubbed her hands together in unmasked glee. "As long as I'm there when Richard sees it, my life will be complete."

Richard was less tolerant of Leatrice's creative wardrobe choices and smothering attention. At one point he'd hoped to influence her style but had given up when she'd worn a Christmas tree skirt complete with dangling electric plug. Kate was right. He would officially blow a gasket if he saw his tiny Yorkie in a dog version of a Leatrice outfit. It would be epic.

"Have you learned anything good from your meddling this time?" Kate asked. "Tell me there was a good reason you chased Jeremy through a rice field aside from providing entertainment to the rest of us."

I made a face at her. "Aside from the fact that he said that both victims deserved what they got and then threatened my life?"

"I'm not saying that's not juicy, but why was he so worked up about Veronica and Dina? I understand he's a diva, but what's his motive?"

I filled Kate in on Jeremy's Inspire connection then reached over to the nightstand, grabbed a bottle of water, and took a swig. "He knew both women and wanted to get his revenge; he got himself added to this trip when he wasn't invited; and he was missing right before Veronica dropped dead. Plus, he was on the beach around the same time Dina was when she died."

Kate steepled her fingers and pressed them to her lips. "I dislike Jeremy as much as anyone, but I feel like a lot of people had a connection to the victims from Inspire. Don't you think Sasha's motive is better? A jilted woman is way more vengeful than a guy who gets dropped from a social group."

"If Jeremy was a regular guy, I'd agree with you, but he's a narcissistic diva. And you know how important it is to him to be seen as a power player."

"True. I wish we had some sort of hard evidence. All of this feels like guessing."

I took a gulp of the room-temperature water, then stood up and walked to the open sliding glass door. "What we need to do is find out how the drinks got poisoned. Someone had to have seen something. We know that Dina's waiter was given a written order to deliver the drink and say it was from Carol Ann. But who told him to say that? And whoever put the poison in the glasses had to come in contact with them between the time they were made and the time the victims took a drink."

Kate scooted to the edge of the bed and dangled her legs over the side. "This definitely sounds more like the meddling you're not supposed to be doing."

"Doesn't it freak you out that two fellow wedding planners have dropped dead on our first overseas FAM trip?" I asked.

"It's not the greatest way to kick off a trip," Kate said. "I'll give you that. At least we aren't the ones who put this entire trip together. Can you imagine spending months arranging everything and then it's all ruined because people keep dropping dead?"

"Actually, I can't." I knew Carol Ann was devastated over the deaths and that this would ruin her fledgling business of promoting resorts to event planners before it got off the ground. It wasn't great news for us, either, since we'd just gotten ourselves on her list. I'd hoped that this trip would turn into many more trips, but it looked like the entire operation would be going down in flames along with my dreams of jet-setting to exotic wedding locales.

I felt a fresh rush of anger over the murders. Who did this person think they were, poisoning wedding planners and ruining people's lives? And over what? Reputations? Infidelity? I slapped my hand against the metal edge of the glass door. "Whoever it is isn't going to get away with it."

"So what are you saying?" Kate slid off the bed and came over to me.

"I'm saying we need to find out for sure who's behind all of this mess," I said, walking to the glass-and-metal railing of the balcony and leaning my hands against it. I spotted Brett and Kristina below us inside one of the fabric-draped cabanas. Brett hadn't been comfortable at the thought of Jeremy being the killer and had nearly squirmed in his seat when I mentioned it. Was that because he actually thought the man was innocent, or did Brett know more than he was telling me?

"If you ask me, we should tell the hotel security team or the police what we know and let them handle it." Kate joined me at the railing and peered over the side. "At least tell them what happened with Jeremy. He did threaten you, after all."

"You're right," I said. "I still think Jeremy is involved in this somehow, otherwise he wouldn't try to scare me off."

"Maybe he's protecting Sasha," Kate suggested.

I shook my head. "I doubt Jeremy would go to the mat for anyone but himself. He's using Sasha just like he uses everyone else."

"What if it's the other way around?" Kate asked. "What if Sasha's using him to distract from her scheme to kill the women? What if he's her fall guy?"

"I like the way you're thinking, Kate. Very devious." I nodded. "I'll definitely tell the hotel security guys what we know about Sasha and Jeremy. That way they can question them. We already know that Jeremy isn't amenable to being questioned by me."

"It looks like Brett and Kristina are heading inside." Kate pointed to the two LA planners as they walked from the pool deck into the lobby. "We should probably start getting ready for dinner soon."

I glanced inside at the digital clock beside the bed. "You're right. After how Mack and Buster teased it to us, I'm excited to see how they've decorated the villas for tonight's party."

"What does 'unforgettable pool decor' even mean?" Kate asked.

I shrugged as I heard a loud knocking on my front door and crossed through the sitting area to open it. Richard stood in the hallway with a cell phone in his outstretched hand. "It's for you."

I stared at the phone then at Richard's solemn expression. Not a good sign.

CHAPTER 18

"So it wasn't Reese?" Kate asked as we stepped out of a golf cart in front of the resort villas, and she straightened the plunging neckline of her pale-blue handkerchief dress. Knowing Kate the way I did and considering her high hemline, there was a distinct possibility that her dress was literally two handkerchiefs stitched together.

I stepped out next to her, releasing my long, flowing skirt and letting it swirl around my ankles. While Kate was showing lots of leg (not to mention plenty of everything else) in the dress she'd chosen for dinner, the only thing exposed in my brightly patterned dress with halter-style top were my bare arms and half of my back. Even though the sun had barely set, and the early evening still held the warmth of the day, I rubbed my arms out of habit, hoping I wouldn't regret leaving my pashmina in the room.

"I never said it was Reese." Richard smoothed the white pocket square tucked into his Wedgewood-blue linen jacket and plucked a nonexistent piece of lint from his white pants.

"I assumed when I saw your facial expression that it was Reese calling to scold me," I said.

"My face was so grim because I'd been talking to Leatrice." He sighed. "Did you know she's knitting hats for Hermes? Hats?"

Kate raised an eyebrow. "I didn't even know Leatrice could knit."

"It takes a very particular face to pull off a hat. I, for instance, look amazing in hats." Richard gestured to me. "You, not so much."

I ignored his snarky comment because he was in one of his 'states,' and I made it a point to give my friend a wide berth when he needed to rant.

"I don't need to tell you all that I have a head made for hats," Fern said, twisting his black beret that looked suspiciously like one of the Balinese police hats. Coupled with his black cargo pants, black lace-up boots, and stone-colored short-sleeved shirt, Fern's homage to local law enforcement was only missing a badge and official patches. "You're all welcome to borrow my udeng if you'd like."

"Your what?" Kate asked.

"My udeng. The Balinese cloth hat I've been wearing." Fern sighed. "I'm starting to think I'm the only one who researched Balinese costumes before we arrived."

"I'm starting to think I'm trapped in a Balinese soap opera," Kate muttered.

"I'm sure Hermes will look fine in the hats," I told Richard as I walked up the wide steps to the entrance.

Richard shook his head at me as he followed. "Annabelle, he's a dog. Dogs should not wear hats, period. I don't want to make him weird."

"You carry him around in a leather satchel. The same leather satchel you named him after, I should add, when you changed his name from Butterscotch to Hermes. I don't think the hats are the issue."

Richard held the tall wooden door open for me. "He's much

too sophisticated a dog to be named Butterscotch. He needed a designer name."

"My point is the hats won't make him odd. You should be happy that he's being taken care of by someone who loves him enough to knit him clothes." I thought about Leatrice fussing over the tiny little black-and-brown Yorkie and felt glad that she had him to take care of while I was away and she couldn't meddle in my life. Worrying about my marriage prospects and trying to figure out why things had never "worked out" with Richard even though he spent a significant amount of time at my apartment usually took up so much of her time that it was good she had Hermes to fill the void.

Richard paused to think about what I'd said then nodded. "You're right. I'm getting all worked up over nothing. It's not like we have to add the hats to the repertoire when I get home. If he insists on them, I'll take him shopping for a nice fedora as a replacement."

Not exactly what I'd meant, but at least he seemed to be letting it go. I'd take the win.

Fern gave a low whistle as we stepped into the marble-floored living room of the main villa. Cream-colored sofas and chairs were arranged around square beige columns that rose up to the high ceilings. In front of a wide wall adorned with a swirling three-dimensional spiral stood a tall octagonal table of polished wood. On top of the gleaming wood were masses of flickering candles perched on high glass holders over low compotes of lush white flowers. The far wall, a series of sliding glass doors, led out onto a terrace with more neutral furniture.

Three Balinese women in long, embroidered skirts and aqua tops tied with ikat-patterned belts greeted us with smiles, their palms together in a prayer pose. I put my hands together and returned their shallow bows. They swept their arms wide to indicate that the guests were outside.

"This way," I said, hearing the low buzz of chatter and music coming from the terrace.

We passed through the living room and onto the terrace where most of the guests were gathered, drinks in hand. Kristina and Brett were sitting on an overstuffed couch talking with Alan, and Cliff and Ted seemed to be trapped in a corner with Chatty Cathy on one side and two illuminated decorative cones on the other. I spotted Sasha and Jeremy, heads together in conversation, as they stood at the glass balcony away from the crowd.

"Isn't this lovely?" Carol Ann asked as she approached us, a waiter following behind holding a tray of premixed cocktails. Her pupils widened slightly as she took in Fern's outfit.

He winked at her and smoothed the front of his snug-fitting shirt before heading off into the crowd, his black boots rapping against the marble floors. I just hoped his outfit wouldn't startle an already edgy crowd.

"The villas are even bigger than our suites," Kate said, taking one of the highball glasses from the tray.

Carol Ann nodded. "These are where the really high rollers stay."

I eyed the cocktails before deciding that the likelihood an entire tray full of drinks had been poisoned was very low. I took a tentative sip of the drink, enjoying the tartness of the citrus blend after so many fruity tropical concoctions over the past few days.

"Have you met Topher and Seth?" Carol Ann asked as she waved over two men I didn't remember seeing before. "Their flight out of New York got delayed, then they got stuck overnight in Amsterdam, so they just arrived today."

The taller of the two men had brown hair touched with gray at the temples and a stylish amount of stubble. He extended his hand. "Seth with Saint Events."

"And I'm Topher." The other man had chocolate-brown wavy hair and eyes that matched behind square-framed hipster glasses. "The T in the Saint."

"I get it. S plus T is the abbreviation for saint." Fern swatted at Seth's arm. "Very clever, boys."

The two men smiled warmly and laughed. I liked these guys already.

Topher watched Carol Ann as she flitted away to another group, then he leaned in to us. "I heard things haven't been going so well."

"Not unless you consider a body count to be a good thing," Richard said.

"Poor Carol Ann," Seth said. "She's been working so hard to launch this FAM trip business."

"Who do you think is behind it?" Topher asked Richard.

Richard had been eyeing the men warily since they'd walked up, but I could see his usual reserve and competitive nature thawing when Topher asked for his opinion.

"We're letting the police handle things," Richard said, giving me a pointed look.

"But the two women were friends, so it's hard to imagine the deaths are unconnected," Kate added, hooking her arm around Topher's as a waiter invited us downstairs for dinner.

"There's a lower level?" Fern asked, following the crowd down an outside marble staircase.

I put a hand on Richard's arm when we reached a landing in the stairs. "Look at the pool!"

Below us stretched a long rectangular pool with the words 'Eat,' 'Pray,' and 'Love' bobbing on the surface in brightly colored letters. Lights shone from above, illuminating the blue water and the floating words. I knew that Bali's tourism had surged since the popular memoir had been published, so a nod to the famous book set in Bali didn't surprise me.

"That must be the pool decor Buster and Mack mentioned," Kate said, twisting around in front of me.

"How did they match the font from the book cover?" Richard asked, clearly impressed.

"And what are they made of to float like that without drifting off to the side?" Fern said.

I leaned over the staircase. "They must be tethered to the bottom with weights. What a fun idea."

Topher turned around and caught Seth's eye. "We should try something like this in New York."

"Way ahead of you," Seth said. "I'm already figuring out how we're going to find the designers and get all the details."

"We can hook you up," Kate said. "The guys who are doing all the design work are friends of ours from DC."

"Really?" Topher said, looking over the top of his glasses. "I always forget that DC has decent talent."

I put a hand on Richard's arm as I felt him bristle next to me. "Take it as a compliment," I whispered. "You know New York is usually ahead of the curve."

When we reached the bottom of the stairs, we walked to an open-air terrace much like the one above us. While the one we'd come from had been filled with lounge furniture, this one was set with a single table stretching from end to end. In contrast to the neutral decor in the cocktail area, the long table was covered in an orange cloth with a lush runner of hot-pink-and-orange flowers filling the center and spanning the entire length. As I got closer to the table, I could see that each place setting featured a gold-beaded placemat and a pink napkin wrapped with an ornate gold ring. Miniature gilded birdcages sat above the napkins and held orange tags with names written in gold.

"No wonder Buster and Mack were so excited about tonight," I said, running my fingers over the smooth beads of a place mat. "They've really outdone themselves."

"Would your designer friends consider coming to New York for an event?" Seth asked.

"We're getting bored of the New York designers," Topher added.

"If they traveled to Bali, I'm sure New York wouldn't be an issue," Kate said.

"Buster and Mack used to work in New York," I reminded Kate as I bent down to look inside the small cages for my name. "Until Jeremy ran them out of town."

Topher grasped my arm. "I'm sorry. What did you say?"

I looked down at his hand, surprised at the firm grip. "That our friends used to have a floral design studio in New York."

"Not that part." Topher shook his head. "Who ran them out of town?"

"Jeremy Johns," I said. "Do you know him?"

Topher released my arm and exchanged a dark look with Seth. "Oh, we know him all right. He spread some not-nice rumors about us a couple of years ago. The best thing that ever happened to us was when he disappeared from the event scene a little less than a year ago."

I did some mental calculations and figured out that Jeremy must have left the New York event market after our disastrous experience with him during our yacht wedding in DC. "Then you're not going to like what I'm about to tell you."

"He's here," Kate said, glancing around her.

I ignored the fact that Kate had stolen my thunder as Topher and Seth gaped at Kate then back at me. "It's true. He's on this trip with a Long Island planner called Sasha."

Topher's hands clenched into fists by his side. "Then he'd better hope he doesn't run into me because I will wring his neck."

I gave a nervous laugh as people looked over at our group. Topher's outburst had not been quiet. "It's probably not the best idea to joke about killing someone after everything that's happened."

"He's not joking," Seth said, his face as contorted with anger as Topher's. "Jeremy Johns had better watch his back."

CHAPTER 19

"W hy is it that the only two people we've ever known to like Jeremy have been brassy women with crazy red hair?" Kate asked, referring to Jeremy's former client and our former stepmother-of-the-bride.

"We do seem to know a lot of people who despise him," I admitted, running my eyes down the table to locate the hated designer. I saw an empty seat beside Sasha but didn't see Jeremy.

We'd taken our seats at the table after a thorough search of the small gold birdcages. Kate sat next to me with Richard across from us, while Fern was at the other end of the long rectangle between Carol Ann and Topher. Seth and Topher had managed to calm down enough to be seated, but one glance down the table at Topher told me he wasn't over it. Seth was seated next to Chatty Cathy a few chairs down from me, but his chair was also vacant. Not that I blamed him for taking a few minutes alone before Cathy talked his ear off the entire dinner.

"So, what do you think?" Mack slid into the open chair beside me and the delicate bamboo groaned from his weight.

I was about to tell him I didn't know what to think about Seth and Topher's feud with Jeremy, but then I realized Mack wanted my opinion on the decor he and Buster had created for the dinner.

"Stunning," I said, meaning every word. "You and Buster have outdone yourselves."

Kate leaned across me. "Seriously gorgeous."

Mack smiled and his face flushed so that it nearly matched the red of his goatee. "The pool decor was my idea."

I put my hand over his and squeezed. "It's inspired." I glanced down the table and saw that Seth had reappeared. "You don't happen to know two planners from Saint Events in New York do you?"

Mack slipped his pink napkin out of the gold ring and draped it across his leather pants. "Topher and Seth? Sure, they were rising stars when Buster and I were closing up shop and moving to DC. Nice guys."

"Well, they're here," Kate said, motioning to where they were sitting. "They had some flight issues getting here, but they arrived today while we were up in Ubud."

Mack craned his neck to see to the end of the table. "I wonder if they remember us after all these years."

"I'll tell you who they do remember," I said. "Jeremy."

Mack's face darkened, reminding me that he and Buster still held a grudge against Jeremy Johns for trashing them all over New York and forcing them to leave town. I knew that if the Christian biker florists allowed themselves curse words, they'd use them all on Jeremy.

"He did the same thing to Seth and Topher that he did to you and Buster," Kate said. "But more recently, so it's still fresh in their minds."

"Jeremy is a cockroach." Mack spat out the words. "No matter what happens he manages to survive, even though he should have been squashed years ago."

Kate shook her head. "It really is amazing someone hasn't pushed him in front of a bus by now."

I shushed Kate, hoping no one had heard her. I didn't want the story of how we knew Jeremy and why we had such bad blood with him to circulate through this crowd since it involved us and another murder investigation.

I sat back in my chair as a waiter placed a white bowl with a wide flat rim in front of me. The ceramic rim was punched with small holes, leaving a small depression in the middle. I read the menu card explaining the glistening golden jelly topped with tiny black orbs: king crab ice jelly topped with caviar. I glanced across the table at Richard who already had a bite of the first course in his mouth, his eyes closed in apparent pleasure.

Mack nudged me. "You don't think all the courses will be this small, do you?"

I eyed the elaborately arranged bite of food in my bowl. "I'm not sure, but there are ten of them." I'd wondered how I'd manage to eat ten courses when I'd first scanned the menu card. Now I knew. "Haute cuisine is about the design of the food and the flavors more than the volume."

Mack scooped up the crab jelly and caviar onto his fork. "Down the hatch."

I followed suit, placing the entire course in my mouth. The sweetness of the crab combined with the sharp saltiness of the caviar as I chewed. I swallowed, taking a sip of cold white wine to wash it down. I was surprised by how much I liked the dish, despite the congealed texture.

"Where is Buster?" I asked Mack as I set my fork in the empty bowl.

He leaned back so I could see Buster's large form a few seats away wedged between Kristina and Brett. I tried to catch his eye, but he was deep in conversation with the two LA planners. I ran my eyes over the rest of the guests, noticing a few empty chairs. Chatty Cathy wasn't at her seat, and I felt relieved for Seth that he'd get a few minutes reprieve while she powdered her nose. I couldn't find Alan in the group but I thought I'd spotted him at cocktails. The seat next to Sasha remained empty. I wondered if Jeremy had decided to skip dinner after realizing Topher and Seth had arrived. It wouldn't have been hard for him to overhear them threatening him.

The terrace buzzed with the sounds of people talking and silverware hitting china as waiters cleared the first course. Now would be the perfect time for me to talk with hotel security about Jeremy's connection to the two victims. Especially since Jeremy wasn't around to overhear me.

I stood up, setting my napkin to the side of my beaded placemat since I intended to return, and made a beeline for Carol Ann. She and Fern looked up as I approached.

"Annabelle!" Fern's face was slightly flushed, and I noticed a waiter in a black vest refilling his empty wine glass. "Carol Ann may let me take her blondee."

My eyes flitted to the woman's curly brown hair, and I cringed at the thought of her as a platinum blonde. I'd seen the transformation of my nutty neighbor's hair from Wayne Newton black to electric burgundy to Marilyn Monroe blond, each change more shocking than the last.

"But Carol Ann has such pretty hair," I said, touching my hand to her bouncy curls.

Fern waved away my protest. "She's ready for a change. Something bold and life changing."

Having Fern bleach her hair until it was the texture of cotton candy would definitely change her life.

I grasped Carol Ann's hand and pulled her up. "Before you boldly go where no hairdresser has gone before, do you mind if I steal her for a moment?"

Fern made a pouty face but took a swig of wine and turned to talk to Topher and Dahlia.

"Is everything okay?" Carol Ann wore a worried expression. "I tried to seat you next to your friends."

I smiled at her. "Everything's great, and the first course was actually delicious. Mack may need a dozen more to get full, but that's another matter. I wanted to see if you could introduce me to the head of hotel security."

"Why?" Her eyes grew wide. "What's happened?"

"Nothing's happened, but I wanted to tell him some things I've learned that might help with the investigation. I don't want to be accused of withholding important information."

Carol Ann let out a breath. "Of course." Her eyes scanned the open terrace. "I know he's around here somewhere, but he's probably trying to be inconspicuous."

"Is he the guy in all black over by that marble column?" I asked, pointing at a Balinese man with a somber expression.

Carol Ann nodded as she led the way over to him and made introductions. One of his eyebrows went up when Carol Ann explained that I had evidence in the murder cases.

"Not evidence," I corrected her. "Some information about the victims and someone who might have wanted to get revenge on them."

The man motioned for us to walk further out of earshot of the dinner, and I noticed a few of the guests shooting curious glances our way. I laid out what I'd learned about Jeremy Johns and his relationship with Dina and Veronica. I closed by relaying what Jeremy had said to me when I'd confronted him about knowing the women.

"He really said they got what they deserved?" Carol Ann put a hand to her mouth and shook her head. "It does sound like he was glad they were dead."

The head of security unfolded his arms. "Where is Mister Jeremy now?"

"He should be at the dinner," Carol Ann said.

I shook my head. "I don't think he ever sat down. The chair next to Sasha has been empty the entire time, and I didn't see him after cocktails."

Now it was Carol Ann's turn to raise her eyebrows. "Why would he disappear?"

"He might have overheard Topher and Seth," I admitted, although I didn't want to say anything that might make the two New York planners look bad. "They weren't too thrilled to find out Jeremy was a fellow attendee."

Carol Ann sighed. "This is a mess. I never should have allowed Sasha to bring him. Actually, I didn't allow it. I had no idea until he showed up with her. I never should have allowed Cliff and Ted to add Sasha to the list. Come to think of it, they added Dina and Veronica, too. If I hadn't taken any of their additions, none of this would have happened."

I didn't respond to that since I was almost certain the *Insider Weddings* guys were the ones who'd gotten my crew added to the list.

"We'll track down Mr. Jeremy and take him to the police for questioning," the head of security said, his dark eyes holding mine. "I'm sure he's still on property. Perhaps he returned to his room."

I felt relieved at the prospect of Jeremy being taken into custody. Neither Richard nor Reese could be upset with me now. I'd given my information to the authorities so they could handle it, and I planned to let them take it from here on out. I thanked the hotel security officer before Carol Ann and I returned to the dinner.

Mack and Kate stood up as I reached my chair.

"We're going to check on the pool installation," Mack said. "The wind is picking up, and I want to make sure it doesn't detach from the bottom."

Kate looped her arm through mine. "Come with us. Mack's going to explain how they did it."

I rubbed my bare arm as I felt the breeze. The second course hadn't yet appeared, and I didn't relish the thought of being left at the table with the two people on either side of me missing. "Okay, but let's make it quick. I don't want to miss the lobster in croute. That sounds heavenly."

We walked from the terrace around the corner to where the pool came into view.

Mack pointed at the marble staircase. "Can you two walk to the landing and tell me if the letters are still even?"

Kate and I walked up the marble steps and paused at the landing, turning so that we had a perfect view of the long, illuminated pool.

"They're even," Kate called down to Mack, "but there's an extra letter at the end."

I felt goose bumps prick my arms as my brain registered the dark form floating at the end of the hot-pink 'e' at the end of 'love.'

"That's not a letter," I whispered, clutching Kate's arm to keep me steady. "That's a body."

CHAPTER 20

"**D**o you think the person is dead?" Kate asked, stepping back from the edge of the stairs, her hands over her ears.

It was hard to hear her over Mack's high-pitched shrieks, but I could read her lips.

"Well, I don't think they're swimming," I said when Mack paused for a breath, working hard to keep the exasperation out of my voice. I felt light-headed as I made my way back down the stairs, holding tight to the cool metal railing to keep from sinking to the ground and hearing Kate's heels slapping against the stone steps behind me.

I kept my eyes lowered so I wouldn't have to see the lifeless form in the water as it bobbed facedown with arms stretched out to the side, but I knew the image wouldn't leave my mind anytime soon. I pressed a hand to my mouth to keep the bile down, wishing the last thing I'd eaten hadn't been crab jelly and caviar.

When Kate and I reached the pool level again, people had begun to gather around Mack, whose piercing shrieks had morphed into cries. I took a deep breath of the cool night air to calm myself before I joined them.

"Who is that?" Mack flung a thick arm in the direction of the pool.

I shook my head, although I knew in the pit of my stomach who was floating in the water. I'd known the instant I'd seen the bright lights illuminating the fanned-out hair.

Fern ran up to us, his black beret slipping off his head. "Don't tell me that's . . ."

"Jeremy Johns," Richard said with a gasp as he reached us. "I'd know the cut of that Armani suit anywhere."

Leave it to Richard to identify a dead body by the designer suit it wore. I'd recognized the blond hair that Jeremy usually styled in a sweep over one eye, which now looked like spun gold as it spread out on top of the blue water and was illuminated from below by the interior pool lights.

The hotel security team scurried around us until one man finally lowered himself into the water, wading out to the body and touching a single finger to Jeremy's neck to confirm that he was, in fact, dead. I could hear a few women crying behind me, but I didn't turn to see who they were. The only person on this trip who had liked Jeremy was Sasha, and she did not strike me as the type to shed a tear over anything. I suspected anyone who was sobbing over the dead designer was doing so to get attention.

Richard draped his jacket over my shoulders. "You're shaking."

"Thanks." I pulled it tight around me, noticing my teeth chattering. I pressed them together, but my body still shook. "I'm going to sit down."

I pushed my way through the murmuring crowd, passing Cliff and Ted with stricken faces and Dahlia, who had an arm wrapped around the doubled-over form of Carol Ann. I sank onto the nearest chair at the now-empty dinner table, and Richard sat down next to me.

"I'd just finished telling the head of hotel security why I thought Jeremy Johns should be their chief murder suspect," I said. "I guess I was a little off base on that."

Richard put a hand on my knee. "We all thought he was the most likely killer. I wouldn't beat yourself up too much."

"At least I was right about one thing. Jeremy was definitely connected to the first two victims. And connected so much that the real killer wanted him dead."

Alan appeared from around the corner, his eyes scanning the area until they found me. "There you are." He came over and bent down between me and Richard, causing Richard to shift his knees and give Alan a death glare. "You all right?"

I smiled at him. "I'm fine. I am getting a little tired of finding dead bodies, though. Have the police arrived yet?"

"Only one, I think." Alan pointed to Fern, who faced away from us. "If I didn't know better, I'd say you were a bit of a corpse magnet."

I didn't tell him how close to the mark he was, but I gave Richard a cautionary glance as he opened his mouth then shut it again.

Alan stood. "Let me get you something to drink. You look parched."

"As long as it's not poisoned," I said with as much of a smile as I could muster.

"You spoil me." Alan winked as he headed off toward a group of huddled waiters.

Richard moved his knees back into place. "Is it me, or is he a bit smothering?"

"It's you."

Richard frowned at me. "He's a little too attentive, if you ask me."

"I'm not his type, if you ask me."

He looked over his shoulder to where Alan had walked. "Really? Interesting. Maybe he's not so bad after all."

I arched an eyebrow at him and held out my hand. "That was a quick change of heart. Now can I borrow your phone?"

He narrowed his eyes at me. "Why?"

"I know you have it on you, and I know you have an international calling plan." I flicked my fingers in a beckoning motion. "Don't play coy with me."

He reached over and slipped his hand inside the pocket of the jacket draped over my shoulders, producing his silver iPhone and holding it out to me on his palm. "I'm going to let this slide since I know you get bossy around crime scenes."

I took the phone from him and stood, squeezing his shoulder. "Thank you. I'm sorry for being bossy."

He crossed his legs and leaned back in his chair. "Luckily for you, I find your overbearing tendencies charming."

I brought up a list of recent calls and redialed the last number called, shooting Richard a look as I walked a few feet away. I guess I shouldn't have been surprised this was his most recent call considering I'd recently outed him as a spy.

"What did she do now?" Reese asked when he answered the phone, clearly thinking he was speaking to Richard.

"*She* didn't do anything," I replied, giving him a beat to recognize my voice.

"Annabelle?" Reese asked. "Why are you calling me from Richard's phone?"

"Don't you mean from your mole's phone?" I asked, tapping my shoe against the stone terrace.

Silence.

"Well?" I asked.

"If you're expecting me to apologize for enlisting your best friend, and one of the few people you listen to, to keep you from getting yourself into more danger, then you're going to be waiting for a long time, babe."

I spluttered for a moment, then fell silent, unnerved by his logic and by him calling me 'babe.' It was the first time he'd used a term of endearment, and I felt glad he couldn't see me flush in response.

"I'd hoped he wouldn't crack under the pressure so soon," Reese said with a sigh.

"He let it slip by accident," I said. "And because he was upset with me."

"Dare I ask why?"

"Because I suspected Jeremy's involvement in the first two murders, and I insisted on trying to get to the bottom of it. You'll be happy to know he tried his hardest to stop me."

"Did it work?" he asked.

I shrugged. "Yes and no. I told the security team everything I knew about Jeremy, including my theory that he killed the two victims."

Reese let out a breath. "That's a step in the right direction. Now let them take it from here."

"But it doesn't matter what I told them." I heard my voice quiver. "We just found Jeremy floating facedown in a swimming pool. My number one suspect is now victim number three."

"Are you telling me another person was murdered?" Reese's voice rose. "So that's three people in as many days?"

"I guess," I said, trying to blink back tears as they stung the back of my eyes. "And now I'm back to square one with no idea who's behind all of this."

"Annabelle." Reese had steadied his voice. "You do not need to figure out who's behind all this. That's the job of the police."

I looked up at the dark sky and blinked rapidly to staunch the tears that threatened to ruin my composure. "But I don't know how good the Balinese police are. I haven't even talked to a detective yet. I don't think they have a lot of murders on the island."

"Do I need to have Richard knock you over the head and put you on a plane back to DC?"

I touched a hand to my head. "You want me to leave in the middle of all this?"

"Yes, I do." Reese's voice had grown loud again. "The longer you stay, the more likely you'll become the next victim."

I shook my head. "All the victims were connected. I don't have any connection to that group, aside from the fact that I knew Jeremy."

"You don't need to have a connection if you keep poking around where you don't belong. What if the killer finds out that you're trying to piece it all together? Then what?"

I hadn't really contemplated the killer getting rid of me to keep me from learning the truth. Probably because I'd been convinced that Jeremy Johns was the killer and having him taken into custody would solve everything.

"I promise to be careful," I said.

"Promise me you'll drop your one-woman investigation," he responded.

I shifted the phone to my other ear. "You know, the reason I'd called you was to get some of your detective's insights on the case."

He laughed. "You didn't think I was going to help you dive deeper into this mess, did you?"

I had thought I could tempt him with the prospect of an unsolved murder, but I'd clearly misread the situation.

"If it was up to me, you and all your friends would be on the next plane off that island." His voice cracked. "I can't stand the thought of you being halfway across the world, and I'm unable to help you. At least when you do crazy things here, I can keep an eye on you and run interference."

Part of me was touched that he cared enough to worry so much, and the other part of me was furious he felt I needed protecting. It was hard to tell which part was winning at the moment.

"It's sweet of you to worry, but I don't need babysitting," I said. "And when is the last time I did something crazy?"

He paused. "Do you really want me to answer that?"

I probably didn't. "I've got my entire crew here to keep me

safe. You have to admit that Buster and Mack are pretty intimidating."

"Is there any way they'd agree to camp outside your hotel room until you leave?"

"We're only here a few more days," I said, spotting the head of hotel security heading my way. "I'll be home before you know it. Right now I have to run."

"Annabelle, I . . ."

I clicked off the phone, wishing I'd had longer to talk to Reese, and wishing I'd been able to tell him how much better I felt when I heard his voice. The second I hung up, I felt a fresh rush of panic. I tried to calm my nerves as the security officer reached me.

His face was solemn. "You were eager to share your suspicions with me about the victim, miss, but you failed to mention your public altercation with him."

CHAPTER 21

"I s anyone else noticing a pattern here?" Fern asked as we made our way through the thinned-out crowd in the villa.

Most of the guests had been questioned and released long ago. The only people who remained were either material witnesses like Kate and me, friends of the witnesses, or people who were loitering out of curiosity. A few waiters gathered empty glasses from tables and had begun to pull tablecloths off high cocktail tables. Candles had been snuffed out, filling the air with the faint scent of smoke and burned wax, and lights were turned up. The soft background music from earlier in the evening had been turned off. Now the only noises were the muffled clinking of plates in the kitchen and the low murmur of voices drifting up from the pool area where the police still attended the dead body.

"If you mean did we happen to notice someone turning up dead right before or during every dinner? Then yes," Richard said, holding open the heavy wooden door as we filed outside. "That little detail stuck out in my mind."

"Not that." Fern tightened his black leather belt, adjusting the brass buckle embossed with a Balinese emblem that looked suspiciously official. "The pattern of Annabelle finding the bodies and getting questioned at length."

"I didn't find the first body." I lifted the hem of my dress as I walked down the stone steps.

"I stand corrected," Fern said. "You're only a suspect in two murders."

"Annabelle isn't a suspect." Kate teetered on her stilettos down the wide stairs. "Is she?"

"Of course I'm not," I said with more confidence than I felt. "I have alibis for both murders."

"You were with us when Dina was killed," Kristina said as she and Brett walked out of the villa behind us.

Kate turned around quickly, clutching my arm to keep from falling down the remaining steps in her absurdly high heels. "What are you two still doing here?"

Brett shrugged. "Probably the same thing as you. Being questioned by the police."

Kristina adjusted the strap of her black one-shoulder dress, and flipped her thick blond hair to the other side. "I think they saved us for last."

"I'm exhausted and starving," Brett said, sinking down onto the bottom step.

Fern snapped his fingers. "That's right. We didn't finish dinner."

I put a hand to my stomach as it growled in apparent response to the reminder that I'd only eaten one bite of food in the past two hours. Unfortunately, that bite had been congealed crab and caviar, and I'd yet to get the salty taste out of my mouth.

Richard glanced at his watch. "At least room service is still available."

Brett got to his feet as a golf cart swung into the circular drive in front of us. As it slowed to a stop, the door to the villa behind us swung open and Sasha barreled down the stairs and pushed past us.

"It's about time," she said as she sidestepped Kate and got into the idling cart, the chiffon layers of her dress and a perfume cloud trailing behind. "I can't bear to stay here another minute."

"Hey," Kate began to protest.

Sasha waved a hand in the direction of the driveway. "You can take the next one."

Even though there was a seat behind the brassy planner, no one made a move to join her. I studied the woman's face to see if I could detect any trace of sadness that her assistant had been found floating facedown in the pool, but her expression displayed nothing but her usual irritation and disdain.

"We're sorry about Jeremy," Kristina said, breaking the silence as we waited for Sasha's cart to drive away.

Sasha's shoulders twitched as she dug in her purse. "He's been nothing but a liability on this trip. If I'd known, I never would have brought him."

"Known what?" I asked.

"He had feuds with everyone." She produced her long electric cigarette holder and waved it at me without meeting my eyes. "With you." She pointed it at Richard. "With him." She leveled it at Brett. "With him."

I looked at Brett, whose cheeks had colored.

Sasha rapped her long holder on the driver's knee. "I'm not getting any younger here. Let's go."

With a lurch, the golf cart took off down the driveway and disappeared into the darkness as another cart drove up to take its place.

"We're saved," Kate said, heading for the cart as it slowed to a stop.

I glanced over my shoulder to see Alan coming out of the villa.

"I couldn't find you," he said when he spotted me. "I thought you'd gone walkabout."

"Aren't you coming?" Richard asked, sliding into the back seat behind Kristina and Brett.

I assessed the seating arrangements in the cart. I could squeeze in between Richard and Fern, but Alan would have to wait by himself. I shook my head. "You all go ahead. We'll take the next one."

Richard pursed his lips but didn't say anything as the cart took off down the drive.

Alan grinned at me. "Thanks for waiting."

"No worries," I said, looking up at the black sky dotted with stars. "It's actually nice and quiet out here."

Alan joined me in looking up, his hands clasped behind his back. The only sound breaking the silence was the chirping of Indonesian frogs. I knew what was going on behind the heavy wooden doors of the stone villa, but in the quiet of the night I could almost forget the police, the emergency personnel, and the lifeless body of Jeremy Johns.

"You missed Sasha's dramatic exit," I told Alan after a few minutes.

He laughed. "I can only imagine. Did she seem upset about her friend's death?"

"Hardly. She called him a liability."

Alan cringed. "Ouch."

"Exactly. She said he had too many feuds with people on this trip."

"She got that part right, didn't she?" Alan stroked two fingers down his beard. "He stirred up trouble with you and all of your team."

"Not only us. The guys from New York who just arrived, Seth and Topher, hated him." I peered into the darkness, wondering how much longer we'd need to wait for a golf cart back to our part of the resort. "And Sasha claimed that Brett had an issue with Jeremy, but I think she may have been confused."

"I don't know. If Jeremy and Brett had a feud, that would explain what I overheard at cocktail hour."

I snapped my head toward him. "What do you mean?"

Alan took a step back as a golf cart swung into the drive in front of us. "It must have been before you arrived. I was getting a drink at the bar and I saw Jeremy and Brett talking in the corner."

"Talking?" I didn't think I'd seen Brett and Jeremy interact directly at all so far, although Brett had seemed pretty knowledge-able about Jeremy's track record at Inspire.

"Well, it was more like Brett telling him that he knew what Jeremy was doing," Alan said, holding out a hand to help me into the front seat of the cart. "And that he never should have come to Bali to begin with."

I sat down, gathering the fabric of my dress with both hands so it wouldn't drag on the ground and twisting to face Alan as he took the seat behind me. "I think a lot of people felt that Jeremy shouldn't be here."

"But I'll bet not everyone warned him that he'd be leaving in a body bag."

CHAPTER 22

"What's going on?" I asked Kate as we walked down to the hotel lobby the next morning.

Two of the FAM trip attendees I'd yet to meet were standing near the portico next to a pile of suitcases. One of the women, a skinny woman with sandy colored hair pulled back in a loose bun, looked nervous as she dug through her purse.

Kate draped a hand over her forehead and blinked hard. "Who knows?" She scanned the lobby. "All I know is I need coffee. For some reason, Not-Long-For-This-World-Natalie called me this morning."

I cringed. "I must have had my phone on silent."

"That's okay," Kate said. "Let's just say that Natalie won't be calling either of us again until we get back home."

I put my fingers to my temples. "What did you say?"

"I told her that she'd gone over her allotted hours and reminded her that each additional hour is billed at two hundred dollars."

"She hasn't . . ." I began.

Kate held up a hand. "But she doesn't know that, does she?"

She inhaled deeply. "Now I must find coffee. I can smell it. I just can't see it."

I took a breath and could also smell the faint scent of coffee filling the morning air. I looked over the lobby's lounge furniture and low tables, spotting several people enjoying breakfast near the floor-to-ceiling glass walls that opened onto the pool deck. The two center glass panels were pulled back, giving a clear view to the towering statues lining the pool and leading down to the turquoise blue of the ocean. Even though it was still early and the lobby held on to the morning hush, the sun was bright and the sky cloudless. I knew it wouldn't be long before the sounds of people splashing in the pool echoed through the elegant marble lobby.

As Kate slid her sunglasses over her eyes to block the sun and stumbled off to hunt down her coffee, I walked over to the women guarding the suitcases.

"I don't think we've met," I said. "Annabelle Archer with Wedding Belles."

Both women stared at me like I had two heads until the one with short, black, curly hair spoke. "You're the one who keeps finding the victims."

I shifted my weight from one foot to the other and took back the hand I'd extended. "Not all of them."

"You found the guy last night who'd been hit over the head and pushed in the pool," she responded.

I tried to think of a response to downplay what happened, but the woman was right. Instead of being poisoned like the two previous victims, Jeremy had been knocked over the head and pushed into the pool. At least that's what the police determined from the bloody knot on the back of his head and the fact he was floating facedown in the water. Not only had my theory of Jeremy being the killer been torpedoed, but since the killer's MO had changed, I couldn't even be sure it was the same person.

The skinny woman laughed, but there was no mirth in it. "Well, we aren't sticking around to be the next bodies you find."

A van swung up underneath the portico, and a uniformed bellman rushed forward to take their suitcases. Messy bun got into the van without looking back.

The dark-haired woman hoisted a black Prada tote onto her shoulder. "If you see Carol Ann, you can tell her that Stacy and Gwen caught the first available flight off this rock."

I didn't respond. Kate reappeared at my side, her hands wrapped around a to-go cup, as I watched the white van drive away.

"What was that all about?"

"Not everyone toughs it out when the bodies start falling," I said.

"You know," Kate said, taking a sip of her coffee, "we haven't properly celebrated Jeremy's demise."

"Celebrated? That seems cold."

She nudged me. "Come on. That guy was a horn in our side from the moment we met him."

"A horn?" I asked.

"Yes. He was a misery to work with; he torched Buster and Mack's business; he ruined our friend Alexandra's cake business in New York; he trashed us to everyone here; he obviously ticked off someone else enough to get himself killed. This was a not a guy worth mourning."

"Maybe," I admitted, shaking the image of his limp body from my mind. "I just wish we'd been far away when he finally got what he deserved."

I spotted Carol Ann, Kelly, and Dahlia walking toward us. All three women looked like they hadn't slept in days, the dark circles under their eyes betraying the long night they'd had after Jeremy's body had been found.

"At least we have two left," Carol Ann said to Dahlia and Kelly as they joined us, running a hand through her hair that now looked more wild than wavy. I noticed that her Southern drawl became more pronounced the less sleep she got, so now her words dripped out like molasses on a cold day.

Dahlia nodded and gave us a weak smile, her eye twitching. Her knuckles were white where she clutched her Lucite clipboard. Kelly's smile was unnaturally bright and looked almost painful.

"Have more people left?" Kate asked.

Carol Ann started to nod, then paused. "More? Who did you see leave?"

"Stacy and Gwen?" I said, my voice more a question than a statement as I tried to recall the names I'd heard only moments ago. "They said to tell you they got a flight out."

Dahlia made some scratches on her clipboard, crossing off names, I guessed. Kelly patted her boss's arm.

"They're the third pair to leave since last night. Jacob and Katherine were the first." Carol Ann sighed. "I suppose I don't blame them, but I'm pretty sure this is the end of my career planning FAM trips."

"Don't say that," Dahlia's voice cracked, and I wondered if she would burst into tears. The bubbly blonde looked on the verge of a breakdown.

"It's okay." Kelly put an arm around Dahlia's shoulders. "There's still the wedding planning business."

"You seem a lot calmer about this than you were yesterday," Kate said.

Carol Ann winked at us. "The pill Dahlia gave me helped."

Dahlia blushed and whispered, "Half a Xanax."

Kate nodded. I knew that she and her millennial friends had a much more thorough awareness of all the anti-anxiety pills on the market as most of them were on at least one. I chalked it up to the stress of DC.

"I'm surprised the police are letting people leave," I said. I knew from past experience that detectives did not like witnesses to leave town during an investigation. I also knew that the Balinese detective had been very specific the night before when he told me not to leave the country. Of course, I had dozens of witnesses who saw me chase Jeremy across a rice field, so I suspected I was a unique case.

Carol Ann shrugged. "The hotel manager pulled some strings so guests who weren't material witnesses could leave."

"Well that doesn't include us," Kate muttered and took a long drink of coffee.

"Or us," Kelly said, her smile flickering. "Although I can't imagine what else the police could ask us."

I had to agree with Kelly. We'd all been questioned by the hotel security chief and then, when he had arrived, the police detective. It had been hours before we'd been able to leave the villa pool and return to our rooms, which explained why Richard and Fern had still not emerged from their rooms despite promising to meet us for breakfast. As if my thoughts had produced them, I spotted the two men coming around the elevator bank toward us.

"Do you think he has any clothes on underneath that?" Kate asked, raising one eyebrow as she spotted Fern, wearing a teal-and-gold sarong tied high around his chest, exposing plenty of bare leg.

"I'm sure he does," I said with a good deal more confidence than I felt. I could only assume that Richard was so worn out from the night before that he hadn't registered what the man next to him had on. Even though his hair was styled and his tan pants and purple shirt unwrinkled, Richard's eyes looked weary. For someone who believed in 'early to bed, early to rise,' the late-night questioning combined with jet lag seemed to be taking its toll.

"Ta da," Fern said with a muted flourish of his hands.

"You look like you're ready for . . ." I paused to find the right word as I glanced at his beaded flip-flops. "Something."

"We're getting away from this place," he said, crossing over to Kate, taking her coffee out of her hands, and taking a swig.

"I don't think we can leave Bali just yet," I said. "At least not until the police clear us."

Fern shook his head. "I meant away from the resort. We're taking a field trip up to Seminyak."

Kate's eyes lit up. "I've heard they have great beach bars."

"Who is?" Richard asked, staring at Fern like he'd just noticed the high man bun and brightly colored sarong worn like a halter dress.

Fern waved a hand at all of us, including Carol Ann, Kelly, and Dahlia. "All of us. Anyone. Everyone. I figured this group needed to get away from all the dead bodies piling up around this joint."

I cringed at the mental picture, then looked at Carol Ann, expecting a protest of the idea. I knew the day's itinerary included a walking tour of the resort followed by afternoon tea.

"That's a wonderful idea," she said. "To be honest, the hotel might be happy to see the back of us for a while."

Since nearly every time we'd had an event on hotel property one of the attendees had been murdered, I could see where they'd shy away from activities with our group.

Fern clapped his hands as a large black van swept into the circular drive of the portico. "Our chariot has arrived."

I eyed the length of the shiny new vehicle and then the size of our group. "I guess we'll have a lot of room to stretch out."

Fern shook his head, motioning to a group of people I recognized walking toward us. "I left messages for all the people we like to join us."

"What about Buster and Mack?" I asked. "Don't we still like them?"

"Of course." Fern swatted at me. "The hotel designers were taking them to a Balinese flower market today, so they had to pass."

"We didn't get a message." I gestured to Kate and myself. Luckily we had dressed in bathing suits under our sundresses and had our beach bags packed for a day we'd originally intended to include plenty of time by the hotel pool.

"I might have forgotten to tell you about the message," Kate said, avoiding my eyes.

"Crikey." Alan rubbed his eyes as he sidled up next to me. "Very early messages."

"You know what they say about the early bird," Kate said, looking much more awake after her coffee, but still avoiding my glare.

Richard gave her a sideways glance. "Do you?"

Kristina ran a hand through her blond hair, resting her sunglasses on top of her head as a headband. "I was told to be downstairs and ready for a trip to a beach with bars." She raised a hand to her eyes to block the sun as it shone through the windows into the lobby. "You had me at 'bars.'"

"What about Brett?" I asked.

Kristina shrugged. "He wasn't feeling so hot."

Fern gave a knowing nod. "Bali belly. Not the kind of thing you want to experience in a public restroom."

I wondered if it was really an upset stomach or if it had to do with Jeremy's death and his earlier argument with the man. Unless I wanted to break down his door, I'd have to wait to find out.

Fern directed everyone to the van, his hands above his head like a flight attendant pointing out exit doors. I hung back as I spotted Cliff and Ted hurrying across the lobby with two women I didn't know in tow.

"Do you think it's okay if we add Grace and Sarah to the group?" Ted asked, pushing his sideswept bangs out of his eyes.

One of the women had brown hair pulled back in a neat bun, and the other woman, a brunette with dip-dyed dark blue ends that fell loose around her shoulders, looked to be around Kate's age. They both had friendly smiles that I recognized from previous events.

"Of course," I said, hoping I wouldn't have to sit on Richard's lap because of my answer. "The more, the merrier."

Cliff leaned close to my ear as he passed. "You're a lifesaver. I didn't want to leave two Editor's Circle members behind."

I followed the foursome into the van, taking the last open seat next to Ted as the Balinese driver slid the door closed behind me. Fern was already holding court in the back seat between Carol Ann and Dahlia, recounting some of his wildest tales from our weddings. I hoped he would stop short of mentioning the other murder investigations we'd been involved in.

"So how many members of the Editor's Circle are on the trip?" I asked Ted, clutching the front passenger's seat where Richard sat for balance as the van accelerated up the driveway. We'd recently gone through the application process to become members of the exclusive group, but I hadn't studied the guest list to see which other members were on the trip with us.

Ted twisted his head to look at the rest of the passengers. "Grace and Sarah, whom you just met. Carol Ann, of course. You and Kate."

"Were any of the victims in the Circle?" I asked.

Ted's usually wide smiled faded. "Just Dina."

"Sasha wasn't?" I asked. "Then are you close friends with her?"

Ted cocked his head at me. "Why would we be close friends with Sasha?"

Cliff turned his head to join the conversation. "We barely know the woman. She's not exactly Editor's Circle material."

"Then why did you add her name to the guest list?" I asked.

Ted put a hand to his chest like I'd stabbed him. "We did no such thing. The only names we put on the list were Circle members like you."

"I must have misunderstood. Sorry." I sat back against the seat.

Cliff gave a nervous laugh. "No worries, but let's nip that rumor in the bud before it spreads."

I glanced behind me at Carol Ann, who was in the back

laughing at one of Fern's exaggerated stories. Why had she told me Cliff and Ted had added Sasha to the guest list if they hadn't? And if she'd lied to me about that, what else was the trip organizer lying about?

CHAPTER 23

I took off my leather flip-flops as I stepped onto the beach, my toes sinking into the gritty sand. Shielding my eyes from the sun that sat high above the ocean, I looked at the wide strip of beige sand stretching in both directions. White-capped waves broke against the shore as children shrieked and chased them back out, while a group of surfers bobbed on their boards further out.

I followed our group as we tramped across the hard-packed sand, passing a series of restaurant bars until we reached one with brightly colored beanbags extending onto the sand and reggae music playing from a pair of speakers. Equally colorful umbrellas adorned with dangling tassels created a canopy over the beanbags.

"This is heaven." Fern flopped down on a beanbag chair and let his head loll back.

The rest of us followed suit, dragging beanbags over until we'd created an amorphous grouping of the lumpy chairs with small wooden end tables interspersed. I sat on a lime-green chair, trying not to flip over on my back as I sank into the squishy center. I pulled the elastic band out of my hair, shaking it out and letting it spill down my back.

Richard sat down in an orange beanbag next to mine, crossing his legs in what I recognized as an attempt to be dignified. Kristina took a chair across from mine, dropping her beach bag in the sand.

"Is Bali supposed to have that much traffic?" Kristina asked, lowering her oversized tortoise-rimmed sunglasses over her eyes. "What's amazing is that no one uses their horn. In LA, people would be laying on their horns."

It had taken us over an hour to reach Seminyak from our resort in Nusa Dua, a distance that a crow could fly in half the time. The roads were surprisingly congested with cars and vans driving bumper-to-bumper and motorbikes swerving in between, yet none of the drivers seemed agitated. It seemed the only people irritated were the Western passengers.

I watched the waves crash and took a breath of the salty air to release the tension of the drive. "It was worth it to get away from the hotel."

"I'll drink to that," Kate said from where she sat between Fern and Alan. "Speaking of drink, they do serve booze here, right?"

Fern held up a brown hard-backed menu. "I'm ordering a La Plancha Breeze. Anyone else?"

One of the women who'd come with Ted and Cliff pointed to an empty pink beanbag next to me. "Do you mind if I sit here?"

I patted it. "Of course not. You're Grace, right?"

I'd guessed at the name, hoping I'd get lucky with a fifty-fifty shot, but she smiled and nodded.

"That's right. Grace Goodwin Events from Chicago." She shifted on the chair as it rolled under her. "You're Annabelle Archer, right?"

"That's right," I said, wondering if Wedding Belles was gaining national exposure or if I was becoming infamous within the group for stumbling onto dead wedding planners. I had a feeling it was the latter, so I didn't ask.

"You're new to the Editor's Circle, aren't you?" Grace asked, taking the menu as Fern passed it to her.

"We've been in it a few months, I think." I motioned to Kate as she tugged the hem of her sundress. "The other half of Wedding Belles."

Grace's eyes widened as she glanced at the menu. "When the price is 90K, that isn't anywhere close to ninety thousand dollars, is it?"

I pulled up the currency convertor I'd downloaded to my phone and tapped in a few numbers. "It's about six dollars."

Grace let out a breath and laughed. "That's a relief."

We ordered drinks from a young waiter in denim shorts topped with a yellow-and-red-batik-print shirt. I watched him as he walked to the open-air building behind us that housed the bar and kitchen. The building was two levels and painted a few different shades of green. The ground level held the bar and a few tables against a wooden rail while the upstairs was filled with tables and chairs in a rainbow of colors shaded by bright tasseled umbrellas like the ones around us on the sand. If everything wasn't so brightly colored, it might have looked dingy and run-down, but instead the vibe was fun and bohemian.

"How long have you been a part of the Circle?" I asked after I'd turned back and set the menu on one of the low wooden tables.

"Almost as long as Ted and Cliff have had the magazine," Grace said. "We go way back."

"So did you know some of the other planners on the list before this trip?" I asked.

Grace crisscrossed her legs in front of her, brushing some sand off the bottom of her white capris. "A few from the list and a few from Inspire."

I leaned forward, trying not to pitch over into the sand. "So you knew the victims then?"

"I knew Dina and Veronica pretty well." She wrinkled her nose. "Jeremy, not so much."

I took the rocks glass filled with a crimson-colored concoction as the waiter handed it to me. The sides of the glass were cold and slick with condensation and felt good against my warm fingers. I took a sip, recognizing the flavors of peach and dragon fruit from the drink description.

"I wouldn't say that I was friends with Dina or Veronica, though," Grace added, sipping on her Kir Royale. "And I definitely was not part of that little clique."

"I've heard about the clique," I said, not wanting to sound judgmental but hoping to get more information out of her. "It sounds interesting."

"I think you mean awful," Grace said. "I'm grateful I never got sucked into that scene." She wiggled a platinum wedding and engagement ring set on her finger. "I'm a happily married woman."

"Were Dina and Veronica?" I asked, picking up my LaPlancha Breeze, although I was pretty sure neither had been.

Grace shook her head. "They weren't, and once they got done with Marilyn, she wasn't either."

I nearly dropped my cocktail in the sand. "Who is Marilyn?" My mind raced through the names of attendees I'd met. "Is she here?"

Grace took a long drink of her bubbly. "No. She hung out with Dina and Veronica at all the Inspire conferences. And Jeremy for a while, although I don't remember if Jeremy was part of the crew when everything went south."

I noticed Richard leaning over so he could eavesdrop on my conversation with Grace, and I shot him a look as he nearly slipped and face planted in the sand.

What? he mouthed as he righted himself and readjusted his beanbag.

I directed my attention back to Grace. "When you say things went south . . .?"

"I thought everyone had heard this story." Grace shot a look over her shoulder, giving me the sense that even if everyone knew the story, no one talked about it. "It's really quite tragic."

I looked down and realized that I'd drained my glass without noticing, so I set it back on the table. "I'm assuming Marilyn was a wedding planner?"

Grace gave a bob of her head. "From Texas. A really sweet woman, but a bit naive considering that she was married with two kids. But maybe that was part of the problem. She'd gotten married young and been with her husband for something like fifteen years. Not that I'm making excuses, but I really did like Marilyn."

Our waiter scooped up my empty glass, and I ordered another round. Grace continued to sip from her thick-rimmed champagne flute.

"Did she have an affair?" I asked as Richard scooted closer to me.

Grace gnawed on her lower lip. "I don't think she even would have considered it if Dina and Veronica hadn't been encouraging her. I think they thought it was a lark. After all, they'd both messed around at Inspire."

I remembered the story of Veronica stealing Sasha's boyfriend, but I wondered whom Dina had been involved with. "So they pushed this Marilyn woman into an affair at an Inspire conference?"

Grace tossed back the rest of her sparkling wine cocktail. "With a photographer from Atlanta who was pretty notorious for making the rounds. I'll admit that he was a charming guy and definitely knew how to sweep a girl off her feet. Marilyn didn't stand a chance."

"And if you ask me, Dina and Veronica set the whole thing up with the photographer." Grace's face flushed; I wasn't sure if it was from the conversation or the bubbly. "I think they wanted to see if he could talk her out of her panties."

Out of the corner of my eye, I could see Richard shake his head in disapproval.

"They don't sound like very good friends," I said, taking my new cocktail from the waiter.

"To be fair, I think they felt bad about it. Afterward. But by then it was too late."

I felt my stomach tighten. "What do you mean?"

"The affair may have been no more than a one-night stand, but Marilyn's husband found out."

I heard the sharp intake of Richard's breath beside me. "How?"

If Grace was startled to hear Richard's voice, she didn't let on. "I'm not sure. She might have confessed. She was the type of person who wouldn't have been able to live with a lie. She was sweet and naive like that."

"I'm guessing her husband didn't take it well?" I asked.

Grace's face twisted into a grimace. "Not by a long shot. He left her. From what I heard, the divorce was ugly. The children ended up staying with their father."

"What about her business? Is she still planning weddings in Texas?" Richard asked.

Grace gave us a curious look. "Still planning weddings? She died over a year ago. Drove her car off a bridge."

I felt my skin go cold. "She's dead?"

"The police called it an accident since they found a lot of alcohol in her system, but who knows? She'd been depressed since the divorce and losing her kids."

My mind raced. "Do you think this had anything to do with Dina and Veronica's murders?"

Grace picked up the new champagne cocktail the waiter had set on the side table. "I can't see how unless Marilyn decided to come back from the dead and take her revenge on them. It's not like any of her other friends are on the trip."

"Who were her other friends?" Richard scooted his chair closer to Grace.

Grace began counting off on her fingers. "There was Amy from Portland and a couple of women from Dallas. Bree and Colleen, I think are their names. After Marilyn died, none of them came back to Inspire."

"What happened to the photographer?" I asked.

Grace took a sip of champagne and hiccupped, putting a hand up to cover her mouth. "Adrian? He's still working in Atlanta and making the rounds at Inspire. I'm glad he's not here. I was afraid Carol Ann might have brought him along."

"Who did I almost bring along?"

I hadn't noticed Carol Ann weaving through the beanbag chairs until she was next to us. Her eyes were unfocused and her step unsteady. I could only assume she'd already put away a couple of cocktails.

The sun barely peeked above the ocean now, lighting the sky with brilliant orange light and transforming the figures standing at the edge of the water into dark silhouettes. Carol Ann stood with the fiery sunset glowing behind her, making her curly hair look like it was edged in gold.

Grace looked up at the woman, a startled expression on her face. "I didn't see you there."

"Who were you afraid I'd bring along?" Carol Ann repeated her question, her Southern drawl even thicker than usual.

"Adrian," Richard said. "The photographer."

"I invited him, but he had to back out at the last minute," Carol Ann said, stumbling over the edge of a beanbag and righting herself.

"He was supposed to be on this trip?" I asked. "Why did he cancel?"

"He ran his car off the road." Carol Ann shook her head. "The day before we flew out, too, so there wasn't time to book someone to come in his place. I should have known when that happened that this trip was cursed."

"Is he okay?" I asked, noticing the sky darkening even further as the sun disappeared below the horizon.

"He's alive, but in the ICU," Carol Ann said as Dahlia came up behind her and took her by the elbow, leading her back to her beanbag with an apologetic glance.

Richard looked at me, and I knew we were thinking the same thing. What were the chances that all three people involved in Marilyn's scandal were either dead or seriously injured?

CHAPTER 24

"So you didn't ask Carol Ann why she invited Sasha on the trip?" Kate asked as we rode the hotel elevator to the third floor.

"Did you not hear the entire story?" Richard asked as the doors pinged open and we stepped out onto the floor that held our suites. "The photographer who was involved in the Inspire scandal with Dina and Veronica is currently in the ICU."

"I heard that part, but he's also back in the U.S. Dina and Veronica were killed here in Bali. I think it's just a weird coincidence that all three have a connection," Kate said. "And don't forget that Jeremy wasn't part of that scandal, and he was murdered, too."

"True," I admitted. "But he did pal around with Dina and Veronica, though Grace thought that ended before the mess with Marilyn."

"I don't understand any of it," Fern said, his words slurring slightly as he wobbled down the dark wood floor. "What does something that happened at an entirely different conference a few years ago have to do with this FAM trip to Bali?"

"Nothing except some of the same attendees," I said. "And the fact that a few of those attendees knew each other and are now dead."

"What if it's just bad karma?" Fern asked. "Didn't you say that Dina and Veronica ruined some woman's life?" He stopped and clutched my arm. "What if it's a curse? You've seen the scary statues of gods they have here. What if one of the Balinese gods of vengeance got them?"

"A curse?" Richard rolled his eyes. "I don't think Hindu gods are known for poisoning people."

"We don't know that." Fern lowered his voice and shot a look behind us in the dimly lit hallway.

"Welcome back." My butler stepped out of a doorway on the hall smiling. "Can I get you anything, Miss Annabelle?"

I put a hand to my rapidly beating heart. "I didn't see you there. No, I'm fine for now. Thanks."

"It's amazing how they pop out of nowhere," Kate said as we continued down the hall. "Every time I walk out of my room, my butler is waiting for me. I think they must have sensors on our doors."

Richard nodded. "The service is excellent. My butler has run me a bath every night we've been here."

I swatted at Richard. "You make him do that every night?"

"What?" Richard shrugged. "The soaking tubs are fabulous, and he loves doing it. It's a win-win. It's not like I'm asking him to do something crazy like arrange my toiletries in alphabetical order. "

I knew that Richard was partly right. It was their job to attend to the suites, but I'd always had a hard time letting people do things for me. I guessed it came from my years as a wedding planner. Being responsible for taking care of everything and fixing any problems was a hard habit to break, even in paradise.

I paused when we reached the door to my suite. "I'll talk to Carol Ann tomorrow when she's sobered up. Maybe then she can explain exactly how Sasha and Jeremy got on the guest list."

"I wouldn't lose too much sleep over it, darling," Fern said. "We only have one more full day of the trip. As long as we can make it through tomorrow, we can fly home and put the murders out of our minds."

"That's right." Kate's face brightened. "And no one got killed today. Maybe the curse has been lifted."

"There's no curse," Richard muttered.

"I forgot to mention," Kate said, holding up her phone, "I learned something, too."

"About the case?" I asked, opening my bag to look for my card key.

She tapped away at her phone. "Not even close. About a dating app. Sarah Swipe showed me."

"Sarah Swipe?" Richard asked.

Kate giggled. "That's what Kristina calls her because she spends so much time swiping on dating apps."

"Is she the one with the dip-dyed hair?" Fern asked.

Kate nodded. "She showed me how to use a Jewish dating app. When you make a match, the people on the screen dance."

Richard looked at me. "Which one of us gets to tell her she isn't Jewish?"

She swatted a hand in his direction. "I know I'm not Jewish, but Sarah thinks I've been limiting my options."

Sarah clearly didn't know Kate. If there was one thing my assistant didn't do, it was limit her dating options.

Fern clapped his hands. "I love Jewish weddings. You could get tossed into the air during the chair dance."

"The hora," I said. After planning dozens of Jewish weddings, I knew the terminology better than most of our clients.

Kate held up her palms. "Not so fast. I'm just swiping for fun, not to get married. And I'm not sold on the no cheeseburger rule."

"You should put that in your profile," Richard muttered. "And that your favorite food is lobster."

I dug through my beach bag, looking for my key card. Nothing. "I swore I put the key card in this side pocket."

"Don't worry," Kate waved her arms and called out to my butler who was still standing in the hallway. "My butler had to let me in the other day when I forgot my key."

Sure enough, my butler rushed up and swiped at the electronic door pad with what I assumed was a master card, giving me a big grin and waving me into my room with a flourish of his arm.

"Thank you," I said, waving at my friends as they continued to their suites.

I dropped my beach bag on the round table near the foyer after one final, fruitless search for the key card. It must have fallen out on the sand, I told myself. I slipped off my flip-flops and padded into the bedroom, hopping onto the bed and leaning back against the mound of pillows. I hesitated for a moment and then dialed Reese's number. As the phone rang, I rehearsed in my mind what I should say to him. I wanted his detective's perspective on what I'd learned, but I also didn't want him to think I was poking around in the case.

I was a bit surprised when the call went to voicemail, but even hearing his deep, steady voice calmed me.

"Hey, it's me," I said after the beep. "I was hoping to talk to you about what I learned today. And before you get upset, I was not poking around in the investigation. This is information I heard when I was talking to some of the other guests on the trip." I left out the part of me asking questions to get the information, but I did outline what I'd discovered about the connection between the two women and the photographer who was currently in the ICU. I hung up after asking him to call me in the morning. My morning would be his evening, and he'd be off work.

I looked at my phone. I knew I should check in on Leatrice, but I wasn't sure if I was up for it. I steeled myself and dialed.

"Annabelle." Leatrice sounded out of breath when she answered. "I'm kind of in the middle of something."

I was almost afraid to ask. "Like what?"

"I'm almost positive the park where I've been taking Hermes for his walks is also being used as a meet up for spies. I've been watching one man in particular, and yesterday we followed him all the way back to his apartment building."

"That sounds a little bit like stalking," I said.

"It's not stalking if he's a Russian sleeper agent. And I'm pretty sure he is since he lives in the same building as former Soviet spies."

I rubbed my temples. "Should I ask how you know this?"

"From the new book, *Spy Sites of Washington DC*. It's my bible."

"So what are you doing now?" I asked.

"We're in hot pursuit. He just left the park after talking with a suspicious-looking older man."

"Are you sure this is safe?" I asked. "What if he doesn't like being followed?"

"Don't worry," Leatrice said, her voice interrupted by the sound of car horns. "Hermes and I are both incognito."

I closed my eyes. Since Leatrice had been known to wear everything from full flying ace gear to sailor suits, I had no idea what she considered flying under the radar. "Which means?"

"Matching trench coats and fedoras, of course."

"Richard's dog is wearing a trench coat and fedora?" Somehow I didn't think an eighty-year-old with platinum blond hair walking a dog in a trench coat could go unnoticed.

"I've got to go, Annabelle. I think we might have been made."

Big surprise there, I thought, as the phone went dead. I dropped it next to me on the bed and it sank into the down of the duvet. It had been nice to leave the resort and spend time at Seminyak, but I'd had more drinks than I usually allowed myself, and I could feel the hint of a headache looming. The thought of Leatrice running around DC with a dog in a trench coat didn't help matters. I swung my feet onto the floor and headed for the shower, stepping out of my sundress and bathing suit and tossing them on the long marble vanity that stretched to the other end of the bathroom. I opened the glass door of the shower and flipped on the water, letting it warm up for a moment before stepping inside.

The hot water felt luxurious as it pounded against my back and washed away the sand that had managed to adhere to every inch of my skin. I squeezed some of the perfumed shampoo into my hand, lathering it before running my hands through my hair. I leaned my head back, letting the water hit my face and cascade down my shoulders.

When I pulled my head out of the water, I heard a noise coming from my room. I froze, but didn't turn off the water. It sounded like someone was walking through my room, but the way the footsteps hit the marble floor, it sounded like the person had on sandals.

"Kate?" I called out, flipping off the water.

The footsteps stopped, but no one answered.

"Fern?" I remembered that he'd been wearing flip-flops, although I suspected he'd passed out the moment he'd reached his room.

The sounds had stopped, but I could feel the presence of someone in my room. I wiped the water from my eyes and tiptoed to the door of the shower. I could see the cream-colored towel hanging on a hook next to the beige bathrobe, but it was several feet away beside the vanity. Should I make a dash for it in the nude and hope the intruder wasn't my Balinese butler in the middle of turndown service? If it were, we'd both be in for a big surprise.

I took a deep breath to steel myself, then I threw open the shower door and darted for the towel, pulling it off the hook and wrapping it around myself as quickly as I could while turning around. As I started to run for the bedroom, my wet foot slipped on the marble floor and I went sprawling onto the floor. Luckily, my hands caught most of my fall, but my knee hit the marble and a bolt of pain shot through me. As I rolled onto my side and cradled my knee, I caught a glimpse of someone running from the sitting area to the foyer. It happened too quickly for me to register much more than a blur, but I knew it wasn't my butler.

I heard the click of the door closing as I pushed myself up off the floor, hobbling to avoid putting weight on my bruised knee. I tightened the towel around my chest as I opened the front door and stuck my head out into the hall. Empty. Where could they have gone? I went a few steps into the hallway and peered down to the elevator bank, but there were still no signs of the fleeing intruder.

I turned to go back into my room just as the door clicked shut behind me. I stood for a moment, my wet hair dripping water onto the floor and creating a puddle around my feet, before I unleashed every curse word I could think of at the locked door. I looked down the empty hallways and assessed my situation. I was soaking wet, wearing nothing but a towel, and my knee was throbbing in pain. Going down to the lobby for a new key was out of the question. I could try to find my butler, but that meant he would see me like this. Not appealing.

I walked gingerly down the hall and knocked on the door next to mine. No answer. Kate must already be asleep. I sighed, held my towel tighter around me, and hurried to the next suite.

"Not a word," I said when Richard opened the door for me.

His eyebrows nearly disappeared underneath his spiky bangs, but he merely waved me inside his room. I made a beeline for his bathroom, pulling his bathrobe off the hook and putting it on over my towel. When I'd pulled the robe closed and wrapped my hair up in a towel turban, I returned to the sitting room.

Richard held out a glass to me filled with a pale-pink liquid. "You look like you need this."

I took a drink. "How did you get Campari here?"

"I brought my own, of course." He set his own glass down on the wooden coffee table. "Now do you want to tell me why you were running around in the hallway looking like an escapee from a bad porno?"

I lowered myself on the beige sofa, avoiding putting pressure on my bruised knee. "I was chasing an intruder out of my room."

Richard's mouth fell open. "Are you okay? Should we call the police?"

I shook my head. "I banged my knee up, but other than that I'm fine."

Richard stood up and began pacing. "Did you get a look at the person who attacked you?"

"They didn't attack me," I said. "They came in my room while I was in the shower. They may have been looking for something."

Richard stopped pacing. "They were trying to rob you? No offense darling, but you don't have anything worth taking. You never wear real jewelry and all your clothes are off the rack."

"Thanks," I said. "But what if the person wasn't after valuables? What if this is somehow connected to the murders?"

Richard tilted his head to one side. "How?"

"I wish I knew," I said. "People know I found two of the bodies and that I've been asking questions about the victims. Maybe they think I have some information or evidence."

"Do you?" Richard asked.

"No, but the killer might be desperate to make sure I don't. Even so, I don't think they found anything. I scared them off before they got past the sitting area."

"That I can believe," Richard said. "Your running mascara is enough to terrify anyone."

I wiped underneath my eyes and glared at him. "Thanks for the sympathy."

"I do believe I told you not to poke around in this murder business." Richard crossed his arms and tapped his foot against the marble floor. "And if I'm not mistaken, so did your hot cop boyfriend. But did you listen to us?"

I didn't answer that. I knew he was right. My compulsion to

fix problems had gotten me into more than one sticky situation before, but I found it almost impossible to resist. After all, as a wedding planner, I was Miss Problem Solver.

"Fine," I admitted. "Both you and Reese were right. Now what do I do to keep the killer from coming after me?"

CHAPTER 25

"I feel like a new woman," Kate said as she walked up to the entrance to the Cafe where Richard and I stood waiting for a table. "I was out like a light last night and slept like a baby."

"I know," I said. "I knocked on your door."

"Really?" She brushed a flyaway blond hair off her face. "Last night?"

I nodded. "I got locked out of my room. Richard ended up letting me in his room."

Kate shook her head. "You seriously need to get a new key, Annabelle."

I held up the white plastic key card I'd just retrieved from the front desk. "I did, and I asked them to rekey the room so no one else can get in using the old key."

A hostess in a sand-colored dress greeted us and directed us to follow her into the restaurant. Light streamed in from the walls of windows on two sides of the spacious restaurant, although gray shades were lowered on one window to block the brightest glare. We threaded our way around tall marble columns and massive square food stations made from the same cream-colored stone. Chandeliers in black birdcages hung above white marble tables surrounded by chairs upholstered in yellow or celadon green.

"You're worried someone will find your lost key and somehow know which room it opens?" Kate asked, taking a seat at a round table.

"She's worried the same person who broke into her room last night will try again," Richard said.

"Someone broke into your room?" Mack asked, coming up behind us and glancing back at Buster who was lumbering up behind him. "I told you we'd miss all the good stuff if we skipped the beach trip."

I patted Mack on the arm. "It happened after we got back from the beach, and it wasn't what I'd call good stuff." I lifted the hem of my light-pink sundress and pointed to my knee, which had turned purple where it had hit the marble floor.

Kate gasped. "Were you attacked?"

I shook my head and took a seat between Richard and Mack. "I fell when I was chasing them out of my room."

"We should tell someone," Buster said, his face a mask of worry.

I inhaled deeply as a waiter poured coffee into my cup. I wasn't crazy about the taste of coffee unless it had so much sugar and cream it wasn't technically coffee anymore, but I loved the smell. "I talked to my butler last night. Unfortunately, he didn't see anything. He'd left the floor for a few minutes. I also talked to the security chief. They checked the camera and could see someone using a key to access the room, but the person was dressed in all black and wearing a wide hat so they couldn't see the face."

"Well, if the hotel isn't going to do anything about it, then Buster and I can guard your door tonight." Mack sat back in his chair and it groaned in protest.

I smiled at the two men, who were nodding intensely. "I don't think you need to do that. Whoever took my first key can no longer use it, so there's no way they can get into my room."

"I offered to switch rooms with her, but she's as stubborn as ever," Richard said, unfurling his napkin onto his lap with a flourish.

"Why would someone break into your room?" Kate asked. "Do you think they were trying to steal something?"

"They didn't take anything. I checked all the drawers and the closet. It sounded like they were rummaging through things, but nothing is missing." I twisted around in my seat to get a better look at the multiple buffet stations throughout the room as my stomach rumbled.

"Odd," Buster said. "Then they didn't find what they were looking for."

"That's what Richard and I thought, but we can't imagine what I might have that someone would want desperately enough to break into my room while I was in it."

"Break into your room?" Fern asked over a plate stacked high with croissants, mini éclairs, and small fruit danish. "What's going on, honey? What's happening?"

"Did you get here before us?" Richard eyed Fern's plate.

Fern set his plate down at the last open seat. "No, but I decided to kill two birds with one stone and make a plate while the hostess led me to your table." He shot us all a look. "And thank you very much for waiting for me."

"On that note," I said, standing up, "I'm going to get some breakfast."

"Right behind you," Kate said, pushing back her chair and following me.

I walked past a station displaying Japanese food on large marble slabs. As much as I loved sushi, I wasn't used to it first thing in the morning. I smiled when I reached the vast display of French pastries set out in wicker baskets and arranged on multi-tier stands. Now this was my idea of comfort food. I grabbed a plate and selected a chocolate-drizzled croissant.

Kate plucked a plain croissant out of a basket. "Have you thought about calling Reese about this?"

"I tried to call him last night, but he didn't pick up. I left a message telling him about the weird coincidence with the photographer and his connection to the two women who were killed. I thought he might have been able to lend some of his detective expertise, but he must have been working."

"He hasn't called you back yet?" Kate asked as we walked from the pastry table to the buffet station with the American selections.

I placed a strip of crispy bacon onto my plate, then broke off the end and popped it into my mouth, savoring the flavor as I chewed. "It's fine. I'm sure he's busy."

"Did you tell him about the break-in?" Kate asked, placing a hash brown wedge onto her plate.

"Nope, that happened after I called him." I wasn't sure if I wanted Reese to know about the break-in. He would probably panic and become convinced I was in mortal danger. Besides, there wasn't much he could do from half a world away except worry.

"You'd better hope Richard doesn't rat you out," Kate said.

I definitely hoped Richard did not tell Reese I'd been running around the hall of our resort wrapped in nothing but a towel. Come to think of it, I hoped he wouldn't be telling anyone that detail.

"Look in here." Kate pointed at a room off to the side with a huge glass wall inset with dozens of colorful glass sculptures. In front of the wall was a long marble buffet inlaid with glass cases filled with delicate desserts. On top of the marble sat even more sweets: rows of colorful macarons, small compotes of chocolate mousse, daintily decorated petit fours.

"I think I'm going to need a second trip," I said, looking down at my full plate.

Kate led the way back to our table. "I'm going back for those chocolate truffles."

"Did you try the ones in our rooms?" I asked as I put my plate down on the table and looked around. It looked like everyone had visited different stations. Mack and Buster had plates filled with sushi while Richard had a bowl of soup and some sticky Chinese buns.

"What ones in our rooms?" Kate asked.

I sat down and draped my napkin over my lap. "The box of chocolate truffles in our rooms."

"What truffles?" Richard asked, and then took a bite of his sesame seed-topped bun.

I looked at him. "The ones in the clear plastic box on our coffee tables last night. The ones with the tags that read 'sweet dreams.'"

Kate shook her head. "I didn't get any chocolates."

I looked at Fern and Richard, then Buster and Mack. They all shook their heads.

"So I'm the only person who got them?" I asked, feeling a chill run down my arms. I tried to remember if the box had been there when I'd gotten back from the beach, but I'd gone straight to the bedroom. I'd only noticed the pretty box with its fancy tag after I'd had my locks rekeyed last night.

"That's not fair." Kate stuck out her bottom lip. "Were they good?"

"I didn't eat them. I was too tired and stressed about the break-in." I took a sip of orange juice and tried to dismiss the nagging feeling in the pit of my stomach.

"Thank goodness." Richard put down his fork. "I don't think the person who broke into your room was trying to take something. I think they were leaving something."

"Leaving some . . .?" Kate started, then stopped herself. "You think there's a reason Annabelle was the only person to get chocolates?"

184

I swallowed hard. "I think we need to go get those truffles and have them tested."

"Tested?" Fern dropped the cheese danish he'd been holding back on the plate.

Richard's expression looked grim. "For poison."

CHAPTER 26

"What are you doing?" Kate asked as she and Fern stood over me, blocking most of my sun even though she wore nothing but a tiny black bikini and a diaphanous white cover-up that barely reached mid thigh.

I sat up in my lounge chair and peered over the top of the paperback I'd been reading. I'd selected a lounge chair that was sitting in the shallow edge of the pool and away from the busier cabanas, so I could dangle my feet in the water and avoid the splashing children. The sun was high in the cloudless blue sky, and I merely needed to turn my head to see the wide stretch of turquoise ocean. "Enjoying the pool. Getting some sun. Relaxing. We are in Bali, after all."

I leaned over and took a sip from the long straw in my frozen lychee martini. The pale-green drink swirled above the rim of the oversized martini glass like soft serve ice cream, and I made a point to sip it slowly to avoid a brain freeze and because the tart drink had quite a kick.

"For one, you never lay out." Kate motioned to my pale legs. "You'll burn within half an hour. And for another, you never let an investigation go."

I picked up my bottle of sunscreen and squeezed some of the sticky, coconut-scented cream into my hand then rubbed it on my arms, the cool lotion feeling good against my warm skin. "SPF sixty. Bullets couldn't get through this stuff. And as for the murder case, I guess I'm finally agreeing with Richard and Reese. I'd rather not be the fourth victim."

Fern sat on the end of my chair, his wide-brimmed straw hat with the word "Diva" stitched across it blotting out any remaining rays. "What about the chocolates of death?"

"I gave them to the head of security," I said. "I'm assuming they'll pass them along to the police to be tested. Regardless, there's nothing I can do about it."

Kate cast a look over her shoulder but the nearest person sat several feet away. "You aren't nervous that the killer might have tried to make you the next victim? That they might try again?"

I held up a finger. "For one, I can't be certain that's what happened. We're jumping to a lot of conclusions by assuming the truffles were poisoned. For all we know, the rest of the group got them and yours were accidentally overlooked."

Fern shook his head, his saucer-like hat nearly clipping me. "No one else got them. We asked."

I looked from Fern to Kate. "You asked everyone?"

Kate waved a hand at the pool area. "While you were busy repelling the rays, we stayed in the cafe and caught people when they came down for breakfast."

Fern winked at me. "I might have convinced a waiter to bring us a Bloody Mary or two."

I took another sip from my martini to regain my shattered feeling of Zen. "Even if I was the only one to get the truffles . . ."

"You were," Kate said.

"Even if I was," I sighed, "it was because the killer thought I was getting too close to discovering them. If it's clear I have zero interest in the murders, they won't have any reason to come after me again." I waved a hand at my surroundings and my cocktail. "Hence the pool time."

Fern shrugged. "Stay alive and get some sun? Sounds like a good plan to me."

"Aren't you always telling me to have more fun?" I asked Kate.

She gave me a suspicious look. "I'm not used to you listening to me."

"So here's where the party is," Alan called as he walked around the edge of the pool toward us. "Mind if I join you? I'll shout the next round of drinks."

"Shout?" Kate asked.

"Sorry." He laughed. "Aussie for buy."

I patted the lounge chair next to mine. "Be my guest. We're squeezing in the last bit of R & R before we have to fly home tomorrow."

"I'm crushed the time has flown by so fast." Alan pulled off his T-shirt to reveal a well-muscled and neatly manscaped chest, and I noticed Fern's look of approval.

"I'm just as crushed." Fern tossed his beach bag to the chair on the other side of Alan and untied his sarong to reveal a pair of Spandex boy-leg trunks. He noticed me eyeing them and winked. "They're like the ones Daniel Craig wore in that James Bond movie."

"They're rainbow striped," I said.

Fern looked down at them. "Well, one does want a pop of color. Think of me as a more fabulous version of James Bond."

"Consider it done," I said as Fern adjusted his man bun.

"Here." Alan produced a candy bar in a shiny purple wrapper with the words 'Violet Crumble' emblazoned in yellow from end to end. "Australia's best export, aside from me."

"A candy bar?" Kate eyed it.

"Not just any candy bar," Alan said. "This one melts in your mouth."

Fern took it out of his hands and tore open the the wrapper. "You don't have to tell me twice."

He passed it to me after taking a bite and groaning with pleasure. I took the chocolate bar out of the wrapper and bit the other end. Instead of being soft nugget or caramel, the insides crackled in my mouth and then melted, giving me a rush of sweetness.

"Why don't we have these at home?" Fern asked, taking the candy bar back from me.

Alan grinned. "You'll have to visit me to get more."

"A trip to Australia could be fun," I said, feeling the effects of the sugar rush combined with my cocktail.

Kate waved over a waiter as she stretched out on the lounge chair next to mine, pointing to my lychee martini. "We'll all take a round of whatever she's drinking because it's obviously magic."

So much for my quiet pool time, I thought, as Fern began chatting up Alan while Kate pawed through her beach bag. I glanced around, noticing a group of fellow FAM trip attendees setting out towels in a cabana across the pool from us. I waved at them, and Brett and Kristina waved back, beckoning for me to join them.

I remembered what Alan had told me about Brett's argument with Jeremy. Now would be the perfect time to ask him about it.

"I'm going to swim over and say hi." I pointed to the cabana as I swung my feet into the ankle-deep water and swept my hair up into a topknot to keep it from getting wet.

Kate pulled off her bathing suit cover-up that covered up next to nothing. "I'll join you."

I hurried to lower myself into the deeper water before Kate stood up next to me in her tiny bikini. I inhaled sharply as I sank up to my neck in the cool water, swimming a few strokes to warm up my muscles and get blood flowing. After the heat of the sun, the pool felt freezing.

Kate swam up next to me, her teeth chattering. "It's frigid in here."

"Keep moving," I said, cutting clean strokes through the water, but keeping my head out of the water so my high ponytail didn't get soaked.

We reached the other side of the pool and rested our arms on the edge. Carol Ann lay on a lounge chair with her eyes closed while Seth and Topher sat in chairs across from her.

Brett lay stretched out on a towel on the floor and rolled his head to one side, smiling at us, his teeth gleaming white against his LA tan. "Is it as cold as it looks?"

I stared at my own reflection in his mirrored sunglasses. "Not once you warm up."

Kate bobbed next to me in the water. "Tell me when the warming up happens."

Kristina came and sat on the edge, hanging her legs into the water next to us and leaning forward so that her fluffy blond hair fell around her face. "Can you believe we have to leave tomorrow? I feel like we just arrived."

"We did just arrive," Seth said, running a hand over his stylish stubble.

"At least we made it for the grand finale evening." Topher pushed his square hipster glasses higher on his nose. "It sounds like it's going to be an extravaganza."

"I just saw it listed as 'wedding show' on the daily itinerary," I said. "And I saw that we need to wear all white."

Brett waved a hand in the air. "There's an all-white night on every FAM trip."

"This time the all white is because of the purification cere-mony we're going to be a part of," Seth said, pouring some tanning oil into his palm.

"We had breakfast with the hotel manager this morning," Topher added. "Apparently, we're going to be treated to a tradi-tional Balinese wedding ceremony followed by a purification ceremony by a Hindu priestess."

"So that's why Buster and Mack ran off so quickly after breakfast saying they had a lot to prepare for before tonight," Kate said to me.

"The resort has really outdone themselves," Kristina said. "I'm going to be sad to leave, and especially sad to leave my suite."

"I'm fine with leaving," Brett said, propping himself up on his elbows. "The resort is gorgeous and the island is beautiful, but I'm not a fan of murder on FAM trips."

"Agreed." Kristina scissored her feet in the water. "This was a first for me."

Kate and I remained silent since murders at events were not a first for us.

"It's amazing how much tension there's been considering we're in such a relaxing setting," I said. "And a lot of it had to do with Jeremy."

Seth muttered something rude about him.

"Exactly," I said. "You hated him, we hated him, Brett hated him."

Brett looked over at me sharply. "What do you mean I hated him?"

I tried to assume my most innocent expression. "I assume you hated him since you warned him he might leave Bali in a body bag."

He blinked a few times before his shoulders gave way, and he slumped over. "Okay, fine. I admit it. I'd watched him manipulate people for years at Inspire. Pushing people to do things then sitting back and watching the devastation without any personal repercussions. I thought he was despicable."

His confession startled me. So did Kristina's nodding.

"I felt the same way," she said. "And it was my idea to threaten Jeremy. Brett and I noticed him scheming with Sasha, and we were convinced he was behind Veronica and Dina's deaths. We decided there was no way he was going to get away with it again."

"You thought he was the killer, too?" Kate asked.

"Of course." Kristina pulled her legs out of the water. "He was the only person who made sense."

Brett shook his head. "But I guess we were wrong. We probably shouldn't have tried to take matters into our own hands, but . . ."

"We're planners. We're used to fixing things," Kristina finished his sentence.

"See?" I whispered to Kate. "We aren't the only people who meddle."

I couldn't help but smile as I looked at the two California planners who'd had the same theories we'd had. Even though they were way more glamorous than me, I felt we were kindred spirits. Too bad we'd all been wrong.

Carol Ann bolted upright in her lounge chair causing Seth to jump. "Do you think people will remember anything from the trip aside from the murders?"

"Of course they will." Topher leaned across and patted her leg. "And it sounds like tonight will be one for the books."

Carol Ann rubbed a hand over her face. "You have no idea how many months of hard work went into planning this trip. It was supposed to launch an entirely new division of our company. What resort wants to hire a company to promote them if the guests drop dead right and left?"

"I think it's just bad luck," Kristina said. "Veronica and Dina went on FAM trips all the time and nothing happened to them."

"And you couldn't have known that adding Sasha to the list would mean she'd bring Jeremy and then he'd end up being one of the victims," I said.

Carol Ann swung her head in my direction. "Who said I added Sasha to the list?"

"The guys from *Insider Weddings*," I said, trying to make my tone sound light even though I knew my words weren't. "According to them, they had nothing to do with Sasha being here."

Carol Ann's face darkened and she gave her head a jerk, as if trying to shake something loose. She stood up, her face flushed crimson, and scooped her beach bag off the floor. "I'm not going to sit here and be accused."

As we watched the woman stalk off, Kristina's mouth gaped open. "What just happened?"

Kate looked at me. "Is it just me or did Carol Ann just move herself into the position of number one suspect?"

CHAPTER 27

"That was a bit of an overreaction," Kate said as we swam back across the pool.

Seth and Topher had gone after Carol Ann to try to calm her down, but I doubted they would have much luck. The sweet Southern belle had looked seriously steamed.

I adjusted the straps of my peach halter-style one-piece suit as we approached the lounge chairs where Fern and Alan were lying, eyes closed and faces toward the sun. "Usually people don't get that angry unless they have something to hide."

Kate rested her arms on the ledge of the pool. "I'm with you that she sounded super guilty just now, but I still can't figure out why she'd sabotage her own trip."

I hoisted myself out of the water in one movement, pivoting so that I was sitting on the edge with my legs in the water. The warmth of the sun felt good as it hit my skin, and I stretched my arms behind me and leaned back to get the full effect. Twisting my head around, I noticed Fern's mouth open as he snored softly. I put a finger to my lips to tell Kate we should talk softly.

"I know what you mean," I whispered. "She's talked about

nothing but how important this trip is to launching the new division of her company."

"Unless all of that talk is a diversion," Kate said, keeping her voice low. "It does provide her with a sort of alibi. She could be a wolf in cheap clothing."

"Sheep's clothing?" I asked.

Kate shook her head at me. "Since when do sheep wear clothes?"

I let it slide and focused on the possibility of Carol Ann being the killer. "That would be pretty devious. To create an entire FAM trip as a diversion from your real goal of killing a bunch of the guests?"

Kate pulled herself out of the pool and stood dripping beside her lounge chair before she reached for the fluffy beige towel rolled up at the end. "When you say it like that it sounds pretty messed up. I'm not sure if I can picture Carol Ann as that much of a schemer. Or that much of a psychotic killer. And what's her motive?"

I stood up and waded through the ankle-deep water around my lounge chair until I could sit down. I lay down on the towel I'd draped across the chair earlier, enjoying the heat of the terry cloth and letting the water on my skin evaporate in the sun. Kate stretched out next to me, dropping the straps of her bikini and tucking them into her black bandeau top, although with the small amount of fabric covering her, I didn't think tan lines would be much of an issue.

"There must be a motive we don't know about," I said quietly. "It seems like too much of a coincidence that she managed the guest list, and the people who ended up on it had a shared history that apparently got them murdered."

Kate's eyes lit up as she noticed a frothy green drink on the table next to her. She leaned over and took a sip from the long pink straw "We're assuming all the deaths are connected. It's entirely possible that someone offed Jeremy because he was a nasty person."

I tapped my fingers on the towel. It hadn't occurred to me that the same person might not have committed all three murders, but Kate had a point. Jeremy had plenty of enemies who might have seen an opportunity to get rid of him amid a string of murders. There were even people on my own team who might have considered it.

Fern jerked awake and leaned over Alan, who appeared to still be asleep. "Who are we talking about?"

"Carol Ann," Kate said. "She freaked out when we confronted her about putting Sasha on the guest list. Annabelle thinks she must have a reason to have killed everyone."

Fern's eyes grew wide. "You do? Sweet little Carol Ann? How could anyone with that accent be a cold-hearted killer?"

"We've come across innocent-looking killers before," I said. "Even really good-looking ones you thought could never be guilty, remember?"

Fern shook his head. "Such a tragedy."

"If you ask me, the sweet ones are more likely to be killers." Kate took a long sip of her drink. "All those cheerful Lily Pulitzer patterns and repressed emotions can't be good for you."

Kate could never be accused of repressing herself with her clothes since most of her wardrobe consisted of outfits I considered too tight, too short, and altogether too much.

Fern nodded. "I'm surprised all serial killers don't wear hair bows."

I narrowed my eyes at him. "If we go by that theory, every sorority house at every big Southern university would be packed with serial killers."

"Sounds about right to me," Kate muttered.

Fern tucked a few loose strands into his topknot. "I'm not saying they're all practicing, but the inclination is there. Trust me. I've done enough of their big hair to know."

"Okay." I picked up my slightly melted lychee martini and stirred the contents with my straw. "I guess with that twisted logic we've established that Carol Ann *could* have killed all three people. But we haven't determined why she would have or even how she did it."

Alan's eyes fluttered open. "Am I having a bizarre dream or are you all discussing serial killer sorority girls?"

Fern patted his shoulder and giggled. "Definitely a dream, sweetie."

Alan sat up and looked at the empty martini glass on the side table next to him. "That drink was stronger than I thought. Am I already hungers?"

I sighed. "We were actually talking about the possibility of Carol Ann killing the three victims."

"The trip organizer?" Alan asked, rubbing a hand across his closely trimmed dark beard. "I thought she was cut that her FAM trip was ruined by the murders?"

"We think that may be a ruse to throw us off her trail," Fern said.

I snapped my fingers. "Do you remember how the drink delivered to Dina was supposedly from Carol Ann? What if it really was from Carol Ann after all?"

"So like perverse psychology?" Kate asked.

Alan looked confused. "Does she mean reverse psychology?"

"Maybe," Fern said under his breath. "We never really know."

"Carol Ann was obviously at the dinner the first night, and she had access to the tables before guests arrived, so it would have been easy for her to slip something into Veronica's water glass or the wine that was pre-poured," I said. "And she could have sent Dina the poisoned cocktail."

Kate turned to her side and propped herself up on one elbow. "What about Jeremy?"

I closed my eyes and thought back to the night at the villas. Lots of people had been up from their seats during dinner. I tried to remember what I'd seen when I'd looked around the long table. Had Carol Ann been one of the missing guests?

"What happened to washing your hands of the case?"

I snapped my eyes open at the sound of Richard's voice. He stood behind my chair, his hands on his hips.

"Where have you been?" Kate asked, raising her cocktail to him. "You're missing all the fun in the sun."

Richard cocked an eyebrow at me. "It sounds like what I'm missing is more amateur sleuthing." He glanced at the pale mark on his wrist where his Gucci watch usually resided. "When I left you no more than an hour ago to go get a massage, you were determined to lay out in the sun and forget all about the murders."

"I tried," I said.

"She did." Kate nodded. "When we got here, she was in full sun-worshipping mode. I mean, as much as she could be while wearing SPF one thousand."

Richard's head swiveled to look at Kate. "So are you the one who sucked her back in?"

"Me?" Kate gave him an affronted look. "When have I ever talked Annabelle into doing something she shouldn't?"

"Where should I begin?" Richard asked.

Kate ignored his remark. "We only started discussing the case again because Carol Ann freaked out when Annabelle mentioned adding Sasha to the guest list. I guess she didn't like being busted like that so she stormed off."

Richard scanned the pool area. "When was Carol Ann here?"

"Technically, she was over there." Fern pointed at the cabana across from us then gave Kristina and Brett a finger wave. "Annabelle and Kate swam over while Alan and I stayed here and worked on our tans."

"We were having a lovely conversation until I mentioned Sasha," I said. "Then she ran off and Seth and Topher went after her."

"Well, that explains what I saw in the lobby just now." Richard tapped a finger against his upper lip.

I sat up. "What did you see?"

"Topher was comforting a sobbing Carol Ann, while Seth was with Dahlia and Kelly at the front desk trying to arrange an early flight home for the three women."

"She's leaving before the farewell party?" Alan asked.

"Or making a run for it," I said.

CHAPTER 28

"**D**o you see her?" Fern peeped over my head at the sea of guests dressed in white as they fanned out across the hotel's lawn that abutted the beach.

At one end of the green lawn, a low stage held an ornately carved gold backdrop and a pair of high-backed wooden ceremonial chairs. A collection of neutral-hued sofas and chairs topped with batik-print cushions faced the stage and guests had already begun staking out the best seats. Waiters in white jackets circulated through the crowd with trays of tropical drinks served in hollowed-out pineapples and adorned with colorful paper umbrellas as Balinese music filled the air. The late afternoon light was soft as the sun dipped below the tree line and cast gold over the surface of the ocean.

"She has to be here," I said, inhaling the scent of freshly mowed grass that overpowered the usual scent of salty ocean water that clung to the air. "Topher said she, Kelly, and Dahlia weren't able to rebook their flights home."

Fern gave a low whistle. "Two things I can't believe. One—there aren't any available flights off the island for a week. Two—you actually curled your hair."

I put a hand to the bouncy curls that fell around my shoulders. "You like?"

Fern winked at me. "If I didn't know better, I'd even say you used a styling product."

A woman from the hotel staff walked up to us and swiftly wrapped us in sarongs and lemon-yellow sashes, topping Fern's head with a traditional Balinese hat that strongly resembled a white napkin tied in a fancy fold.

I glanced around and noticed the other guests also getting outfitted. "This must be part of the ceremony."

"I like yours." Fern nodded to my pink sarong, adjusting his forest green one and frowning. "Do you think mine is too subdued?"

"You look great," I assured him, weaving my way across the flat expanse of grass and taking a cocktail from a waiter along the way. "The hat makes up for the dark color."

Fern touched a hand to the hat that perched high above the ponytail at the nape of his neck. "I do love a good hat."

"You're here," Kate said as she teetered up to us in high cork-heeled shoes. "Alan and I were having a hard time chasing people away from our couch."

I saw Alan a few feet away in a burgundy sarong, stretched across the better part of a beige sofa. He waved us over, sitting up as we joined him. "People are frothing for these prime seats."

"So much for keeping track of Carol Ann," I said, resting my pineapple drink on a dark rattan side table.

"Are you kidding?" Kate swept an arm wide. "This is a prime location to watch for her. We're close to the stage and in the center of the lawn."

Fern sank into the sofa. "It's like a very comfortable stakeout. Much better than that one we did in Leatrice's car." He wrinkled his nose. "Do you remember? The nearest public restroom was three blocks away."

I remembered very well and felt grateful that I didn't have to deal with Leatrice and her obsession with amateur surveillance on top of everything else. Knowing her, she'd be hiding in the bushes right now with infrared sensors.

I took a seat next to Alan. "Have you seen Carol Ann yet?"

"No," he said, adjusting the white cloth hat on his head. "But I see Dahlia so her boss must be here as well."

I swung my gaze to follow his, spotting the usually bubbly blond assistant standing unsmiling beside the bar, her Lucite clipboard clutched tightly in one hand. The stress of the trip, the murders, and her hysterical boss had clearly taken a toll. Kelly walked up to her, her cat-eyed glasses glinting in the setting sun, and whispered in her ear until Dahlia nodded. I looked around, knowing that Carol Ann couldn't be far.

"Aren't these delicious?" Grace plopped down beside me as she took a sip from her pineapple. Her dark hair was pulled back into a low bun and she'd tucked a pink orchid behind one ear.

"Be careful." Alan wagged a finger at her. "I think they're deadly. Blow the froth off more than one, and you'll be falling on the floor."

"After this trip, I'm not sure self medicating is such a bad idea." Grace pulled out her phone and began scrolling through her pictures. "I wanted to show you something since we were talking about Marilyn yesterday. I completely forgot I'd saved these."

I sat forward as she held up the screen. I recognized Dina, Veronica, and Jeremy in the photo but not the thin woman with them. "Is that Marilyn, the woman who died?"

Grace nodded. "I guess I'd remembered incorrectly. Jeremy must have still been friends with them when everything went down because this was taken at that Inspire conference."

I took the phone from her to get a better look at the one person in the photo I'd never met. She was pretty, with sandy blond hair that fell to her shoulders, but her smile looked forced. And vaguely familiar. "I feel like I've seen her before. Do you know if she ever did an event in DC?"

Grace thought for a moment. "I'm not sure. Her business was starting to take off when everything imploded around her. I know her husband had political contacts, so she may have planned something for one of their congressmen in Washington."

Alan looked over my shoulder at the photo and shuddered. "Everyone in that picture is dead now."

I stared at the image and felt a chill pass through me. It felt unsettling to look at a photo of smiling people who had all died unnatural deaths. I studied Marilyn's face more closely.

"She doesn't look happy in this photo." I passed the device back to Grace.

Grace glanced at the image. "She was always a bit manic. Most of the time she was up, but she did have downturns."

"I didn't think you knew her well."

"I knew *about* her more than I knew her, but we'd spoken a few times." Grace explained. "You know how it is in the wedding industry. People's reputations precede them."

That was true. Thanks to Fern's love of gossip, I knew things about wedding vendors in DC I'd never even worked with.

"It sounds like Marilyn wasn't the most stable person," I said. "Why would her friends push her into something if they knew she might not be able to handle it?"

Grace took a long sip on her straw, emptying the pineapple and sucking up air. "They may not have understood. Marilyn seemed happy most of the time."

I'd known people with manic tendencies before, and they could be very good at hiding their pain. I felt a twinge of sadness for this woman I'd never known. It sounded to me like she'd been taken advantage of by a group of thoughtless people. Of course, all those thoughtless people were now dead, and unless I was very mistaken, someone was getting revenge for Marilyn.

"Are you sure there aren't any of her other friends on this trip?" I asked.

Grace hiccupped and put her fingers to her lips. "Not that I know of."

"Carol Ann wasn't friendly with her?"

"If they were, they didn't pal around at Inspire."

I sat back against the couch cushions. Would Carol Ann kill three people to take revenge for a woman she wasn't close with? It seemed like a stretch. A thought occurred to me.

"Was she a member of the Editor's Circle?" I asked.

"Carol Ann?" Grace looked at me funny. "Of course."

I waved my hands. "Not Carol Ann. Marilyn."

Grace pressed her lips together while she thought. "Come to think of it, she was. Not for long if I remember correctly, though."

Before I could ask her how well Cliff and Ted knew Marilyn, the music intensified and a murmur passed through the crowd. I twisted to see a procession approaching from the beach. Balinese men in white Nehru jackets carried two wooden litters—one held a beautiful woman in an elaborate gold headdress and matching collar over her colorful dress, and the other held a man wearing a burgundy-and-gold hat and an outfit as brightly patterned as his counterpart's.

"This must be the Balinese wedding ceremony," Alan said, sitting up to get a better look.

Grace had risen from the couch, her phone held up to record the dramatic entrance, and she took a few steps closer to the action. So much for getting more information from her now.

"Can I talk to you?" The voice barely reached my ears over the loud music.

I turned to see Carol Ann standing behind the sofa holding a drink, her eyes darting around the lawn. Kate and Fern had run up close to the processional and Alan was standing and clapping along to the music, so no one noticed as I got up and walked around to join Carol Ann.

"I wasn't sure if you'd come," I said, bending close to her ear so she could hear me.

"I needed to talk to you," she said. "I'm not sure what I should do."

"About what?"

"I know you think I had something to do with the murders." She shifted from one foot to the other. "Because I arranged to get all the victims on the guest list, right?"

"Something like that," I said, not sure where this conversation was going but wishing I wasn't the only person hearing it.

"Well, you're wrong. I didn't put the victims on the list." She ran her eyes over the crowd and raised her pineapple cocktail to her lips.

I caught her wrist before she took a sip, knocking the drink to the ground. She wrenched her arm away from me and jumped back. "What are you doing?"

I pointed to the overturned fruit, its contents leaking into the grass at our feet. "The inside of the pineapple is black."

Carol Ann's mouth opened and closed again as my words sank in.

I knelt down and picked up the pineapple by the bumpy green skin. The yellow inside of the fruit had turned black around the edges, almost like it had been burned. "It looks like someone tried to make you the next victim."

CHAPTER 29

Carol Ann's head swung wildly from side to side as she backed away from me. If this was an act to convince me that she wasn't the killer, it was very effective.

"What were you going to tell me?" I asked over the loud music. The processional had reached the stage and the Balinese bride and groom were being lowered to the ground.

She raised a hand to her throat and gaped at the pineapple in my hands. "My drink was poisoned?"

I peered into the hollowed-out fruit, its pale-yellow flesh dark on the inside. "I don't know for certain, but whatever was in your cocktail was toxic enough to turn the pineapple. We can have the police take it and test it to be sure."

She didn't seem to be listening to me as her eyes darted over the lawn. The Balinese processional made its way to the stage, the bride and groom taking their seats on the ornately carved wooden chairs in the center and the attendants in colorful costumes fanning out on either side. The music changed and the female attendants went out into the crowd, pulling guests up to dance.

Fern ran up to me. "Isn't this spectacular? I'm not sure which outfit I love more—the bride's or the groom's. Which do you think would look better on me, Annabelle?" He took a breath as he noticed me holding the empty pineapple out to Carol Ann and her stricken expression. "Is everything okay?"

"Someone's trying to kill me." Carol Ann's voice sounded shaky.

"I think we all feel that way, don't we?" Fern put an arm around her shoulders. "Maybe you should sit down for a second."

Carol Ann nodded mutely as Fern led her to the nearest beige sofa. As Fern comforted the clearly shaken woman, I set the pineapple on a nearby end table and scanned the crowd for Richard. Where was he?

I caught a glimpse of him across the lawn with a beautifully costumed Balinese dancer as she tried to teach him the exaggerated moves of the traditional dance. It wasn't going well. Richard's version of Balinese dance looked like a cross between "vogueing" and a seizure. I hurried across to him as quickly as I could without running. One of my hard-and-fast rules as a wedding planner? Never run. If the person in charge looked concerned, it made everyone else panic. I kept a smile on my face as I approached him, and I bowed slightly to the dancer as I tugged on Richard's sleeve.

"I'm in the middle of something," Richard said, "and I think I'm almost getting it."

I pulled him away from the dancer with an apologetic look to her. "I'm sorry, but you're not."

He gave me a withering look and stopped swiveling his hips. "Fine. What is it?"

I looked over my shoulder to confirm Fern still had Carol Ann occupied. "The killer tried to knock off Carol Ann."

"I thought your number one suspect for who the murderer could be *was* Carol Ann," Richard said.

"I might be wrong about that." I took his arm and tugged him a few feet away from the nearest dancing couple. "Carol Ann asked to speak to me, but then I noticed that her pineapple was black."

"I'm sorry? Her what was what?"

I pointed to a waiter passing with a tray of cocktails in hollowed-out pineapple glasses. "She was drinking one of those, and I realized the inside of the pineapple, the part filled with the drink, was turning black."

Richard made a face. "That's not a good sign."

"Carol Ann was seriously shaken up when I showed her, and I don't think there's any way she's pretending about that."

"So much for solving the case." Richard crossed his arms across his chest. "Maybe now's a good time to leave it to the police."

"Maybe." I stared at Carol Ann as she sat on the couch, Fern next to her touching up her hair. "She did mention that she didn't add the victims' names to the list. But we already know that the guys from *Insider Weddings* didn't add them, either."

"At least that's what they claim," Richard reminded me.

I thought back to how insistent Cliff and Ted had been about not adding Sasha. They had seemed almost affronted by the thought that they would have included her. "I think they're telling the truth, too."

"I hate to be the one to tell you this, darling," Richard said. "But you can't make both of them right. They were the only ones who made up the guest list, correct?"

I bit the edge of my lower lip. "Yes. From what I understand, Cliff and Ted added some members of the Editor's Circle who weren't on Carol Ann's list, but that was it."

"So either one of the guys from *Insider Weddings* lied and he did add Veronica's and Sasha's names to the list, or Carol Ann is lying and added their names and also tried to poison herself." Richard leaned forward. "I'll bet one of Carol Ann's assistants could sort this out for us in two seconds."

"You're right. Dahlia and Kelly know every detail about this trip." I paused as what I'd said aloud sunk in. "They could just as easily have added names to the list and told their boss that the guys at *Insider Weddings* wanted them on. Carol Ann wouldn't have given it a second thought."

Richard's eyebrows shot up. "You think those two girls are killers? They're barely out of braces and OxiClean."

"They aren't that young," I said to him. "Early twenties."

"Why would they want to murder a bunch of people they've never met?" Richard asked. "At least Carol Ann knew the victims or some of them. Dahlia and Kelly are completely new to the wedding world. Didn't Carol Ann say Dahlia's only been with her a year and Kelly is an intern? I have a hard time seeing the motive even if I could picture them as serial killers."

I threw my hands into the air. "So explain who snuck the victims onto the guest list. The person who made sure the victims were on the list has to be the killer. Why else go to so much trouble? Someone wanted those people to be here on the island so they could poison them. Everyone else on the list was either a member of the Editor's Circle or someone Carol Ann wanted to include. All except Veronica, Dina, Sasha, and Jeremy."

"I still say we ask Kelly and Dahlia," Richard said.

I shook my head. "And tip our hand?"

Richard stared at me unblinking. "What hand?"

"If either one of them is involved with the murders, we don't want them to know that we know." I looked across the lawn for the two blond assistants.

"Don't worry. I don't think you really know what you know, so there isn't much danger of them finding out."

I stifled the urge to stick my tongue out at him. Sometimes Richard's habit of poking holes in my theories made me want to kick him. Especially when he made sense.

"What was it that Carol Ann wanted to talk to you about before you discovered her drink had been poisoned?" Richard asked. "You never told me her confession."

I put my fingers to my temples. "She didn't tell me. We both freaked out a bit after we realized her drink had been poisoned. Fern took charge of calming her down while I came to tell you."

"Where is she now?" Richard looked over my head at the pairs of dancers spread across the lawn.

I followed his gaze until I spotted Carol Ann's curly brown hair. "It looks like she and Fern are taking a seat for the purification ritual."

At the far end of the lawn closest to the sand, rows of white, wooden folding chairs were set up beneath a stage upon which sat a Balinese woman wearing all white with lots of dark hair piled on top of her head. Despite her hair adding a few inches, the woman with coils of gold snaking around her arms was small and thin.

"That must be the high priestess who's here to do the cleansing ritual."

"Didn't we miss the boat on purification for this trip?" Richard looked suspiciously at the woman now kneeling at the edge of the stage, surrounded by attendants holding golden bowls. "I think the fox is already in the hen house."

I grabbed his sleeve, pulling him with me as I crossed to the chairs. "Come on. I want to try to sit next to Carol Ann so I can ask her what she wanted to tell me."

We dodged several people as we wound our way toward the small stage, finally reaching Carol Ann and Fern on the front row. I sat down next to Carol Ann and gave her a quick smile.

"Feeling better?" I asked.

She shrugged, her head bobbing back and forth and her eyes unfocused.

I leaned back and got Fern's attention. "Did you get her drunk?"

He sucked in a breath. "Of course not. She wouldn't touch a drink after her last one was poisoned." He lowered his voice to a whisper. "So I gave her a Valium."

"What?" I tried not to scream, but Carol Ann jumped at the sound of my raised voice.

"Just a half." Fern held up two fingers to show me the size of the half pill. "The woman needed something. She was a wreck."

So much for getting any valuable information out of her, I thought as I watched Carol Ann's head loll forward. I narrowed my eyes at Fern's wide smile. "And the other half?"

He giggled, his cheeks flushing pink. "Waste not, want not."

I stifled the urge to reach across and pinch him. Instead, I nudged Richard next to me. "Fern and Carol Ann are doped up on Valium."

He craned his head around me to look at the two, both with vacant smiles on their faces as they gazed up at the priestess who had begun to chant. "I see no difference."

Before I could agree with him, one of the priestess's attendants waved us forward. I hoisted Carol Ann up by the arm and pushed her to follow Fern as he led our row to the front of the stage. I linked my arm through hers even when we were directed to put our hands in the prayer position and close our eyes. I did not want to open my eyes and find her in a heap beside me.

I could hear the chanting of the priestess growing louder, along with Richard's muttered complaints about voodoo nonsense, before I was suddenly drenched with water. I opened my eyes to see the priestess shaking water over us with a large brush, but closed them again before being hit with another spray,

"She must be out of her mind," Richard spluttered next to me. "Can't she see I'm wearing silk?"

The attendant directed us off to the side so the next group could take our place and get purified.

"I feel renewed," Fern said, squeezing water from his ponytail.

"Well, you look like a wet rat," Richard said, trying to pull his soaking shirt away from his skin.

I wished I'd worn waterproof mascara as I ran a hand over my face, trying to clear the water from my eyes. I could imagine the black streaks trailing down my cheeks. I blinked hard as I spotted a figure coming toward me.

Fern poked me in the side. "It may be the Valium talking, but that guy looks a lot like Detective Reese."

"The tall guy with dark hair?" Carol Ann leaned against me as she squinted across the lawn to follow Fern's gaze. "Does anyone else see two of them?"

CHAPTER 30

"What would Reese be doing here?" I asked, holding up my hand to shield my eyes from the bright shaft of sunlight as it dipped behind the trees. The setting sun put the approaching men in shadows, but I felt a jolt of recognition as I studied the broad-shouldered silhouette with the long, confident gait.

"Maybe it's a mirage," Fern suggested. "I've always wanted to see a mirage."

I could hear the sounds of the high priestess purifying the next group of people behind us—a rhythmic cadence of chanting broken only by the sounds of water being splashed—but the noise blurred into the background as my mind tried to process the unbelievable sight in front of me.

"Did you know about this?" I asked Richard, who was still trying to air-dry his silk shirt by flapping it away from his body.

"About what?" Richard glanced up and froze.

Fern turned to me and inhaled sharply. "Darling, we need to fix your face before you scare this gorgeous mirage away." He produced a powder compact from his pocket and began dabbing at my face.

Kate hurried up to me and tugged at my sleeve. "You're not going to believe who's here."

I waved away Fern's compact sponge as he patted powder onto my chin, my heart beating fast as Detective Mike Reese reached me. I thought about asking him what he was doing in Bali, but then a better question popped into my head. "Did you really drag your brother all the way to Bali with you so you two could check up on me?"

Daniel Reese grinned at me and hoisted a black carry-on bag higher on his shoulder. He was taller than his younger brother but shared the same dark hair, although Daniel's had flecks of gray at the temples. We'd met Mike's brother when he provided security for one of our more problematic weddings. As a veteran of the DC police department, he ran a successful private security firm and employed a lot of former law enforcement officers like himself. Daniel's combination of brawn and authoritative presence was something both brothers shared, though I found him less bossy than his kid brother.

Mike tilted his head at me. "I thought it would take two of us to handle you and your cohorts."

"Handle us?" I put a hand on one hip. "Do we look like we need handling?"

Mike and Daniel looked us up and down, their raised eyebrows telling me that they clearly did believe we needed help. I glanced around me, remembering we were all soaking wet and wearing white tops with colorful sarongs wrapped around our waists. The white Balinese hats Fern and Richard wore, the fabric now soggy and dripping water into their faces, didn't help our case either.

"We just finished a purification ritual," I explained, shooting Kate a look as I noticed how translucent her blouse had become and how hard Daniel Reese attempted to divert his eyes. "Although I don't know how well it took."

The corner of Mike's mouth turned up. "If I'd known you were getting purified, I might have hopped on an earlier plane."

Fern pushed me forward, whispering in my ear, "Now is not the time to play hard to get. Not with the current state of your makeup."

Mike caught me by the elbow as I stumbled a bit. "I had been hoping for a warmer reception."

I looked up at him, feeling my defensiveness melt as I met his eyes and they deepened from hazel to green. "You surprised me that's all."

He leaned down, lowering his mouth to my ear. "That was the point."

"Aren't you going to introduce me to your handsome friends?" Carol Ann asked, her Southern drawl magnified by the effects of the Valium.

I took a small step away from Mike, but his hand remained on my arm. "Carol Ann, this is Mike and Daniel Reese. Friends from DC."

"A pleasure to meet you both." Carol Ann staggered forward, sagging against Daniel who put an arm around her waist to catch her. "I'm in charge of this trip."

I noticed a look of recognition pass across Mike's face. "You're from Atlanta?"

Carol Ann giggled. "Have you been reading up on me?"

Mike didn't answer her, but I knew he'd probably researched all the names I'd mentioned during my phone calls.

"Why don't you and I go sit down?" Kate tried to pull Carol Ann away from Daniel, giving Fern a beseeching look to help her. She might flirt outrageously with men, but she didn't appreciate it when other women did the same.

Fern grabbed Carol Ann's other arm, and he and Kate steered the woman to a nearby couch while she craned her neck behind her, batting her eyelashes at Daniel.

"Fern might have given her half a Valium to calm her down," I said. "She isn't usually so . . ." I paused to find the right word. "Uninhibited."

"Any specific reason why a hairdresser is administering prescription meds?" Mike asked.

"Carol Ann was a bit hysterical earlier," I said, wondering how to bring up the reason she'd been so upset without sending Mike into full cop mode. "And it was only half a pill."

"Can you blame her?" Richard touched a hand to his hair, which had remaining remarkably in place despite the dousing. "If you hadn't stopped her from drinking, she might be victim number four."

I glared at Richard as Mike's mouth fell open.

Richard looked from me to Mike and back to me. "Oops." He backed away. "I should leave you two to catch up."

Mike took a deep breath. "Maybe now would be a good time to catch me up on what's been happening while I've been in the air."

I led both brothers to the beige sofa across from Fern, Kate, and Carol Ann. Close enough to keep an eye on them, but out of earshot. "So how long did it take you to get here anyway?"

"Over twenty hours," Daniel said, readjusting a brightly colored batik pillow behind his back.

I thought back "So you must have left . . ."

"After I got your message about the photographer. That's when I realized you were still poking around and might become a suspect, or worse, a victim. You have a bad habit of implicating yourself in crimes without even trying. I've heard enough about foreign prisons to know I don't want you ending up in one."

"I'll have you know I was never even a suspect." I felt a mixture of annoyance and gratitude. The detective was right. I'd had the misfortune of landing on the suspect list for a few criminal investigations. I wasn't thrilled he'd felt the need to fly halfway around the world to save me from myself, but I did feel relieved to have him sitting next to me holding my hand.

"But you were almost a victim," he reminded me.

"How did you know. . .?" I began before I answered my own question with the obvious. "Richard."

"He's just as concerned about you as I am. And he knows that you can't help your compulsion to solve every problem you encounter, even when it isn't your problem."

"How did he reach you when you were in the air?" I asked.

"We had a quick layover in Taipei," Daniel said. "Just enough time to check messages and get on the next plane."

Mike nodded. "I heard all my messages. I just didn't have time to call anyone back." He squeezed my hand. "In-flight calls are crazy expensive, and I blew everything on the flight over here."

I felt my face flush. "It must have cost you both a fortune to get last-minute tickets to Bali."

Daniel leaned back and cast a glance toward the beach. "There are worse places to end up."

"But we all leave tomorrow," I said. "I hate to think you flew all this way for nothing."

Mike sat forward and a dark curl fell over his forehead. "We didn't fly here for nothing, Annabelle. We came here because we have pertinent information about this case."

I stared at him. "How can you have information about a murder investigation in Bali? I know you're good, but I don't think you're that good."

He smiled at me. "I had Daniel booking our tickets while I was talking to the Atlanta PD. I had a feeling that photographer didn't have a random accident."

I looked around us to see if anyone could overhear, but everyone had gathered near the side stage, preoccupied by watching the purification ritual. "I thought it was a pretty big coincidence, but that would mean that Carol Ann had something to do with his death. She's the only one who knew him, or knew he was supposed to come on this trip."

Mike looked at Carol Ann, who sat across from us, her legs

splayed and her head lolled back against the cushions. "She couldn't have been the only one. She's not blonde."

"What does being blonde have to do with it?" I asked.

"Because witnesses in Atlanta saw the photographer drinking with a young blond woman for hours before he drove off in his car and into a telephone pole."

"Grace did say he was known for being a ladies' man. Are you telling me a woman got him drunk before he got in his car? That seems more like bad judgment than murder."

Mike shook his head. "There was very little alcohol in his system. There was, however, a toxin."

"What kind of toxin?" I asked, holding my breath in anticipation of the answer.

"Ethylene glycol," Mike said, his face somber. "Or what you know as antifreeze."

CHAPTER 31

"You're telling me he was poisoned with antifreeze just like Veronica and Dina?" I tried to keep my voice calm, but I could hear the rising panic make my voice sound shrill.

"It wasn't enough to kill him," Mike said. "But police suspect it made him disoriented enough to run off the road."

I sank back onto the sofa, letting the information settle in my brain. Three people had been dosed with antifreeze and all three were connected to the Inspire scandal. I let my eyes close for a minute, and I breathed in and out a few times to slow my thoughts, which were muddled and chaotic. In the background, I heard the chanting of the high priestess layered over the lapping of the nearby waves as they reached the shore.

"Annabelle? Are you okay?" Mike's voice broke through my deep breathing.

I opened my eyes. "I'm okay. I was thinking." I let my eyes drift over the crowd, seeing Chatty Cathy standing with Seth and Topher next to the bar while Kristina stood a few feet away with Brett, wringing water from her hair. The priestess appeared to be wrapping up her ritual, and everyone seemed to be damp to some extent. Some, like me, had been in the front row and were thoroughly soaked, but others had stayed in the back and gotten a sprinkle. I searched the crowd but didn't see the women I was looking for. "There are two blondes here who are from Atlanta."

Daniel sat up. "And is one of them connected to the victims?"

"Actually, no." I bit the edge of my lower lip. "At least not that I'm aware of. Both of them are pretty young and had never met anyone on the trip until we arrived."

Mike exchanged a look with his brother. "So we've got opportunity, but no motive."

"Where are these two now?" Daniel asked.

I ran my eyes over the lawn. "There they are." I indicated Carol Ann's two assistants with my head. They sat with Cliff and Ted on a long sofa flanked by two matching chairs. Both women looked like they'd gotten the gentle misting version of the purification ritual. "Dahlia is the one with lighter hair, and Kelly has the pixie cut. Did the witnesses in Atlanta describe the woman?"

Mike frowned. "The only descriptor I got was blond. I was lucky to get that much since I had no connection to the case."

Daniel watched the women. "They are young. Are they even out of college?"

"At least one is," I said.

"Who are we talking about?" Fern called to me, leaning over so far he had to catch himself with one hand before he tumbled onto the grass. "Dahlia and Kelly?"

Carol Ann jerked up as if she'd been jolted out of a deep sleep. "My girls? Where are my girls?"

Fern patted her hand. "You just relax, sweetie. Everything's fine. Your girls are enjoying the party."

Carol Ann gave him a vacant smile through barely opened eyes. "It had to be an accident, you know. Neither of my girls would ever try to kill me."

Fern looked at me, a startled expression on his face, then turned back to the doped-up Southern belle. "What do you mean?

You think one of your assistants had something to do with the attempt on your life."

She shook her head vigorously. "Never. They both know I would take their secrets to the grave."

I walked over and took a seat next to Carol Ann, pushing Kate out of the way. "What secrets would you take to the grave?"

Carol Ann swung her head over to look at me and frowned. "You want to get people in trouble."

"No, I don't," I said, trying to make my voice sound as soft and sweet as I could, although I could never match the syrupy sweetness of her Southern drawl. "I want to help keep people safe. Don't you want that, too?"

Carol Ann closed her eyes for a moment, and then they flew open. "You're trying to trick me, aren't you?" She wagged a finger at me. "It won't work. I thought about telling you. I really did." Her eyes looked pleading. "But I can't, and none of your tricks will get it out of me."

Daniel nudged me over and took my place next to Carol Ann, clasping her hand in his. "Would I try to trick you?"

She focused on his face and her face melted into a nauseating smile. "Never."

Daniel returned her smile. "You'll tell me your secrets won't you, honey?"

"Please tell me I don't look like that when I smile," Mike muttered.

"You promise me you won't tell a soul, sugar?" Carol Ann ran a finger down the side of Daniel's face. "I'm sure she didn't mean it."

"Who didn't mean it?" Daniel asked.

"At first I didn't think it could be true." Carol Ann shook her head as if trying to dislodge a thought. "I tried to pretend it was random—that the two murders couldn't be connected. I even thought Jeremy's murder could have been by someone else. So many people despised him, you see. But when you mentioned the names being added to the guest list, and that *Insider*

Weddings hadn't added them, I knew. But I didn't want it to be true."

"It's not your fault," Daniel said, his voice soothing. I wondered how many times during his career as a police officer he'd had to talk people off the ledge.

"But then she tried to kill me." Carol Ann's face crumpled. "Little ole' me. After everything I'd done. I still can't believe it. She must know I'm one of the last people who knows the truth. And knows who she is."

I felt like shaking Carol Ann to get her to say the girl's name, but I restrained myself. I noticed Mike jiggling his knee next to me and realized he felt as impatient as I did.

Daniel put a muscular arm around Carol Ann. "Tell me who it is, hon, and I'll keep you safe."

Carol Ann's pupils widened. "Aren't you the sweetest thing? You know, I've tried to be like a mother to her since Marilyn died. Her mother and I weren't close, but I always felt awful I didn't help her more when her life fell apart. I've tried to make it up to her daughter."

"I'm sure you've been amazing," Daniel said.

"You're a doll to say so." Carol Ann puckered her lips before she collapsed against Daniel's chest.

Kate gasped. "Is she dead?"

Daniel put a finger under her nose, and shook his head. "Just passed out."

"She didn't give us a name," Mike said.

"But we know it's one of two people," Kate said. "Why don't we do eeny-meeny-miney-mo?"

Fern shrugged. "We have a fifty-fifty shot of guessing the right blonde."

"Those are bad odds if you're the innocent one," Daniel said, as he extracted his arm from around Carol Ann.

Fern tapped his chin. "Well, it's either the one with the pixie cut or the one who dyes her hair."

"Dahlia dyes her hair?" I asked.

Fern rolled his eyes at me. "The one with long hair definitely goes blonder than she is in real life. From her roots, I'd guess her real shade is more of a sandy blond."

A recent memory bubbled to the surface of my mind. "Marilyn had sandy blond hair. I saw a picture of her." I turned to Kate. "And do you remember when we first got here and Carol Ann told us how she'd been like a mother to one of her assistants?"

Kate nodded. "It was Dahlia."

"Exactly," I said, thinking back to the tidbits of information we'd heard throughout the trip. "Dahlia had just graduated from college when she started working for Carol Ann which means she would have been a teenager when her mother died."

Fern shuddered. "Are you telling me a teenaged girl planned all these murders to get revenge for her mother?"

"Let's ask her." I turned to where Dahlia had been sitting, but her space was empty. Only Cliff and Ted sat chatting with Kelly.

Kate grabbed my hand. "She's gone."

CHAPTER 32

F ern swiveled his head to search the crowd. "Do you think
she heard us?"

I stood up to get a better look. "She may have seen
us talking to Carol Ann and figured it wouldn't end well
for her."

"She can't go far," Reese said. "We are on an island, after all."

"But it's a pretty big island," I reminded him.

Alan walked up, brushing droplets of water from his short
beard. He stopped when he saw the Reese brothers. "What do we
have here?"

"This is my . . ." I paused for a moment not knowing exactly
how I should describe my relationship with Mike.

"Boyfriend," Kate supplied for me. "And he's a cop from DC
who's here to help us catch the killer."

Alan nudged me. "G'donya, mate."

Mike eyed Alan briefly before turning away to look for Dahlia.
At least he and Richard would have one more thing in common—
their jealousy of my new Australian friend.

"Have you seen Dahlia?" I asked Alan.

"Dahlia?" He turned to sweep the space with his eyes. "I saw her rush across the lawn a few minutes ago. I figured it was a party-planner emergency."

Fern pointed toward the ocean. "Isn't that her running along the beach?"

I followed his finger and saw that the assistant had shed her sarong and was running in white capri pants and a loose white blouse toward the main building of the resort.

I pulled off my sarong, turning back to Mike. "You and Daniel run around the front in case she tries to escape by the main entrance and we'll chase her to you." I waved to Kate and Fern to follow me. "Come on, you two."

Fern stood up and began hopping toward me, flailing his arms like he was in a three-legged race. "This fabric has no give. Go on without me."

I pulled at the sarong, unwinding it from his waist to reveal a pair of white gym shorts that left little to the imagination.

"What?" he said as Kate stared at his short shorts. "You know I don't own much white. It makes me look like a house."

"You look fine," I said, knowing full well I couldn't fit into his tiny shorts even if I used a shoehorn. "Now, come on."

The three of us dashed across the lawn and onto the hard-packed sand of the beach. I slipped off my sandals and felt the coarseness under my toes as I ran parallel to the water.

"She's cutting through the hotel," Kate called to me, hitching up her white minidress so she could go faster and, no doubt, so she could flash more thigh. If anyone could pick up a guy while chasing a suspect, it would be Kate.

We followed Dahlia around the pool, dodging waiters carrying trays of cocktails and swimmers wrapped up in towels. When we reached the glass wall panels leading into the lobby, we stopped short.

Fern bent over and put his hands on his knees as he breathed heavily. "Where did she go?"

I swept my gaze down the long wall of glass. All the panels

were closed, but I could see a flash of blond hair as Dahlia hurried through the lobby. How had she gotten inside?

"Over here." Kate pointed to a tall knobless door to the far right of the glass wall. She pushed hard, and the door swung in, revealing a closet that connected to the lobby.

Fern pushed me into the closet and squeezed in behind me. "Pivot, ladies. The only way out of here is to turn on the spot like you're in a beauty pageant. Twist and pivot."

We twisted and pivoted, pushing open the door on the other side of the glass wall and spilling out into the lobby.

"That may be the strangest connecting door I've ever seen," I said, giving a final glance to a broom that stood in the corner of the closet-cum-passage.

Fern waved a hand in the air. "She's heading for the entrance."

Dahlia looked over her shoulder as she ran under the covered portico and jumped in a waiting golf cart, taking off up the curved driveway.

"She's got wheels," Fern said in a tone of disbelief.

"So do we," Kate said, making a beeline for an empty golf cart and hopping in the driver's seat. I slid into the seat next to her, and Fern got in the back.

"Do you know how to drive one of these things?" I asked as the cart lurched forward, and I grasped the top for balance.

"It can't be harder than driving a car," she replied, gunning it up the drive.

I decided not to mention that her driving didn't often inspire confidence as Fern slid from one end of the back bench seat to the other, catching himself before flying onto the pavement.

"There she is." Kate pointed as we closed the distance between our golf cart and Dahlia's. Luckily Dahlia's cart had a pair of suitcases in the back seat weighing her down, so she wasn't able to surge ahead.

A runner passed us going in the same direction, and I looked down at the speedometer. "Can't this go any faster?"

"Maybe we should ask that runner to grab her?" Fern suggested.

Kate stepped on the gas and soon we were drawing even with the other cart.

"Pull over," I shouted.

Dahlia ignored me, so Kate jerked the steering wheel to the left and our front bumper rammed into the side of Dahlia's cart. She ran off the road for a second, the suitcases behind her toppling over, but quickly righted herself, glaring at us and accelerating toward the resort entrance.

"We're about to get passed again," Fern said.

I looked behind us and spotted Mike and Daniel Reese closing in fast on foot. "This is ridiculous. We might as well be in a white Bronco."

When we caught up to Dahlia's cart again, Kate maneuvered us close enough so that I could reach over and grab Dahlia's steering wheel, but it was Fern's piercing scream as he leapt onto the back of her cart that caused Dahlia to lose control and drive into a cluster of low bushes. The cart tipped onto its side, and Dahlia fell out into the shrubbery with Fern on top of her.

Kate pulled our cart to a stop, but Mike and Daniel reached the entangled pair first.

"Get off me!" Dahlia screamed from underneath Fern, who lay spread eagle on top of her but facing up.

Daniel hoisted Fern to a standing position while Mike grabbed Dahlia and put both of her hands behind her back. Her cheeks were flushed pink and her blond hair fell across her face.

"It was nothing personal," she said when she saw me staring at her.

"The murders weren't personal?" I asked, finding that very hard to believe.

"No. The chocolates I left in your room. I just wanted to make you sick so you wouldn't keep poking around and asking questions."

"So they weren't poisoned?" Kate asked.

Dahlia blew a strand of hair off her nose, her hands still held tightly behind her back. "I filled them with a laxative."

"Thanks, I think," I said.

"I didn't hurt anyone who didn't deserve it," Dahlia said as Mike began to walk her back to the lobby. "All of them were responsible for my mother's death. I just set things right."

"It's still a good thing you didn't eat those chocolates." Kate patted me on the back. "It would have been hard to chase down a suspect if you'd been camped out in the bathroom."

Not a pretty thought.

"Did you see me subdue her?" Fern asked as he picked leaves and twigs out of his hair.

"I thought you were trying to make a snow angel on top of her," Kate said.

"If you must know," Fern said, "I was trying not to be inappropriate."

"Then you shouldn't wear those shorts," Richard said, as he joined us.

"Where did you come from?" I asked, turning to see Buster and Mack jogging up the driveway not far behind him with Alan closing in fast.

Mack stopped to suck in air when he reached us. "You all drove right by the entrance to the lawn, and we heard Fern screaming."

Buster gaped as he saw Dahlia being led off. "Is Dahlia the killer?"

I nodded. "It's a long story."

Mack made a pouty face. "I'm just sorry we weren't here to help tackle her."

Kate thumped him on the arm. "There's always next time."

Alan looked at all of us. "I have to say, I've never met Americans like you before."

CHAPTER 33

"I think I'll walk," I said when Fern asked if I'd like a ride back to the lobby in the golf cart.

"Suit yourself." He threw up a hand in a wave as he peeled off down the drive, Alan riding shotgun with Kate on his lap.

Richard shook his head as we watched them disappear into the dusk. "Five bucks they end up in the bushes again."

"Five bucks Kate and Fern end up fighting over Alan," I said.

Richard wrinkled his nose. "Too many muscles for my taste."

"I hate that," I deadpanned.

I didn't point out that Richard's biggest problem with Alan was probably that the Australian had befriended me. Sharing was not Richard's strong suit. I linked my arm through Richard's, and he gave my hand a brusque pat.

Buster and Mack had dashed off to put the finishing touches on the farewell dinner they insisted was still happening despite having to adjust all the seating since one of the guests would be spending the evening in custody. I wondered if anyone had broken the news to Carol Ann and Kelly, and I felt glad that it wouldn't be me. I didn't think that would be an easy conversation, although it might be a while until Carol Ann was lucid enough to understand.

I took a deep breath and looked up at the sky, which had darkened to a navy blue now that the sun had set. I could smell the frangipani blossoms as a gentle breeze stirred the nearby trees, and I felt a sense of calm pass over me despite the wail of sirens approaching at a distance. The killer was in custody which meant no more bodies and no more worrying about being the next victim. I hadn't realized how worried I'd been until I felt the tension drain away.

"Just so I understand," Richard said, stepping around me so that he walked on the side of approaching traffic. "Why did Dahlia kill everyone?"

"Revenge." I veered into the grass as several gray cars with yellow stripes and the word "Polisi" on the sides swept by us, heading toward the lobby with their blue lights flashing. "Her mother was Marilyn, the woman whose life fell apart after she had a fling at one of the Inspire conferences."

"And Dahlia blamed all the victims for it?"

"From what Grace told me, Dina, Veronica, and Jeremy liked to egg people on, especially when it came to romance."

Richard made a face. "I'd hardly call a hookup at a conference romantic."

"Agreed." I looked behind me to make sure no more police cars were coming before stepping back onto the pavement. "It must have taken the girl years to put it all together and decide who to take her revenge on. She was only a teenager when it all went down."

"Pretty clever to get a job with a wedding planner so she could have access to all the right people," Richard said. "That takes ingenuity and planning. Too bad she's a cold-blooded killer or I'd consider hiring her."

"And she made sure to add the names of her victims to the

FAM trip, telling Carol Ann that they were added by the guys at *Insider Weddings*."

"But didn't Carol Ann know who she was?" Richard asked. "Didn't she think it was a coincidence that these particular people ended up on the trip?"

I shrugged. "Either she was in a serious state of denial, or she didn't know how much information Dahlia knew about what happened with her mother. I feel sorry for Carol Ann. She probably gave Dahlia a job because she felt guilty about what happened to Marilyn, and the girl used her position to go on a killing spree."

"Good help is hard to find." Richard sighed. "What about the person Marilyn had the affair with?"

"The photographer in Atlanta?" I linked my arm through Richard's again so I wouldn't trip and fall in the dark. "He was the first victim, although he's not dead. He was supposed to come on the trip, but maybe Dahlia wanted to test out her poisoning skills on him first. He did just run his car off the road and not go into cardiac arrest, so she must have increased her dosage for the next victims."

Richard shuddered. "Everyone here seemed to die pretty quickly, except Jeremy. She whacked him on the head instead. Not that I blame her."

"I've thought about that murder and why it was a bit different," I said. "I think he knew who she was. Jeremy was always good at getting dirt on people, and I think he either recognized her because she resembles her mother or remembered Marilyn mentioning her name. That's why Jeremy told us someone else on the trip knew Dina and Veronica got what they deserved. He knew who she was and probably confronted her by the pool."

"Then she knocked him over the head when he turned his back on her," Richard said. "I'll say it again. There's a lot to like about this girl."

"And don't forget that the deaths weren't as fast as they seemed. I think Dahlia poisoned both women over a period of hours. Remember that Dina and Veronica had drinks with Carol Ann and her team before the welcome dinner. She could have slipped small amounts of antifreeze in their drinks starting then."

"It would explain why Veronica seemed drunk at dinner. The effects of the poison."

"Exactly," I said.

Richard's phone trilled in his pocket and he pulled it out, looking at the name on the screen and rolling his eyes. "Leatrice. I hope she's not calling me again to ask if Hermes can have Chinese food." He pushed the talk button, listening for a moment before groaning. "What do you mean he's in love? He's a dog."

I raised an eyebrow at him as we reached the lobby and paused beside the large marble entrance table while Richard listened to Leatrice, one hand on his hip and one foot tapping rapidly on the floor.

"I don't care if she's a toy poodle. Dogs don't date." Richard shook his head, and I took the phone from him.

"Hey, Leatrice. It's Annabelle. What's this about Hermes dating?"

"Annabelle." Leatrice sounded relieved to hear my voice. "I didn't say dating. I said that he's set his cap on a pretty little poodle at the park."

"When you say 'set his cap' do you mean that literally? Is Hermes wearing another hat?" I asked. Since Leatrice had told me she and Hermes had matching fedoras, the question didn't seem out of place.

Leatrice laughed. "Of course not. We only wear our fedoras when we're under cover. How's everything going in Bali?"

"Pretty good," I said. I had no intention of telling Leatrice about the murders until I was back on American soil. Knowing how crazy my neighbor was for true crime, I couldn't be certain she wouldn't hop on the first plane over with Hermes in tow. "We should be back the day after tomorrow."

"About that . . ." Mike Reese said as he came up to me.

"Got to run, Leatrice. I'll see you soon." I hung up and handed Richard back his phone.

"I don't think that flight out tomorrow is going to happen," Reese said, glancing over his shoulder to where the Balinese police were handcuffing Dahlia.

"Why?" Kate asked as she and Fern joined us. "Don't tell me the police need to keep us here for questioning. They should be thanking us for tracking down a killer, not ruining our travel plans."

Mike looked at his feet. "It's not them, it's me."

"You're keeping us here for questioning?" Fern asked, giving me a wink. "Not that anyone here would object to a little police interrogation."

"No." Mike smiled at me and flashed a resort card key. "The hotel manager was so grateful she gave us two suites for a week. I thought you might want to stay with me and have an actual vacation."

Fern's mouth fell open. "What do I get? I threw myself on top of a deranged killer."

"Actually, the hotel is extending all of your suites another week," Daniel said as he walked up. "We told them that you all were the ones who figured it out."

Fern batted his eyelashes at Daniel. "Well aren't you a doll?"

"They comped us an entire week?" Richard asked. "I suppose experiencing Bali without the threat of death might be nice."

Mike nodded, flipping his card key over the top of his knuckles. "And apparently our suites are on the same floor as yours."

I looked at the tall, handsome detective who'd flown halfway around the world to make sure I was safe, and I felt all my usual hesitation and caution disappear. I jumped into his arms, wrapping my legs around his waist.

He staggered back a few steps, looking as surprised as I felt. "I guess that means you're happy to see me?"

"You could say that." I leaned down and kissed him, his lips soft and warm against mine. The kiss became more urgent, and I pulled back, breathing heavy, my legs still wound tightly around him.

Richard cleared his throat. "I would tell you to get a room, but you have two of them."

"Now that's what I'm talking about," Kate said, throwing herself against Daniel and pulling him down into a long kiss.

Fern glanced at Richard, who held up a palm. "Don't even think about it."

"I think this is going to be a good week," I said to Mike as I leaned in for another kiss.

FREE DOWNLOAD!

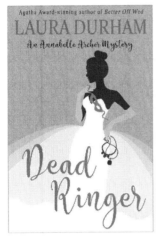

ALSO BY LAURA DURHAM

Read the entire Annabelle Archer Series in order:

Better Off Wed

For Better Or Hearse

Dead Ringer

Review To A Kill

Death On The Aisle

Night of the Living Wed

Eat, Prey, Love

Groomed For Murder (coming soon!)

To get notices whenever I release a new book, follow me on BookBub:

https://www.bookbub.com/profile/laura-durham

Did you enjoy this book? You can make a big difference!

I'm very lucky to have a loyal bunch of readers, and honest reviews are the best way to help bring my books to the attention of new readers.

If you enjoyed *Eat, Prey, Love*, I would be very grateful if you could spend just two minutes leaving a review (it can be as short as you like) on Goodreads, Bookbub, or your favorite retailer.

Thanks for reading and reviewing!

ABOUT THE AUTHOR

Laura Durham has been writing for as long as she can remember and has been plotting murders since she began planning weddings over twenty years ago. Her first novel, BETTER OFF WED, won the Agatha Award for Best First Novel.

When she isn't writing or wrangling brides, Laura loves traveling with her family, standup paddling, perfecting the perfect brownie recipe, and reading obsessively.

She loves hearing from readers and she would love to hear from you! Send an email or connect on Facebook or Twitter (links below) or Instagram (lauradurhamauthor).

Find me on:
www.lauradurham.com
laura@lauradurham.com

ACKNOWLEDGMENTS

This book would never have existed it I hadn't had the amazing opportunity to visit Bali as part of a wedding FAM trip. Thank you to Mary Frances, Walt, and Art for putting together an amazing experience and to The Mulia Bali for hosting us and spoiling us rotten. The descriptions in the book don't come close to how stunning the resort is in real life. If you get the chance, visit Bali and stay at The Mulia!

As always, thank you to my readers and my advance reader/review team. You all have eagle eyes, and give me the best ideas!

My deepest gratitude to my husband and my kids for their support and for not trashing the house when I go to writing conferences (or to Bali). And much love to my parents and extended family—my original cheerleaders.

Printed in Great Britain
by Amazon